inevitable

A Kingpin Love Affair Vol: 2

J. L. BECK

More by J.L. Beck

The Bittersweet Series:
(New Adult Contemporary)

BITTERSWEET REVENGE
BITTERSWEET LOVE
BITTERSWEET HATE
BITTERSWEET SYMPHONY
BITTERSWEET TRUST

A Kingpin Love Affair:
(Dark Romance)

Indebted (Vol: 1)
Inevitable (Vol: 2)

author disclaimer

This book is intended for readers 18+ only. It's a dark, erotic romance that contains copious amounts of violence, sex, murder, swearing, dubiousness, and other things that aren't suitable for a younger audience.

This book also contains graphic abuse, some that may trigger unwanted or hidden emotions. Please be advised that I DO NOT condone this type of behavior, and I DO NOT agree with emotional and/or physical abuse in any way, shape, or form.

This is a work of fiction, and nothing contained in it is based off of my life or someone else's life. Please heed the warning when I say that this is dark. It's not rainbows and ponies; it's murder and darkness that blooms into love.

Dedication

To my daughter—Annabella. You're mommy's angel. I'm sorry for all the SpaghettiOs, TV dinners, and Lunchables you have to eat. This is for you! Xoxo

table of contents

prologue

Bree

My ears rang with the sound of a gun being shot reverberated through my mind. Zerro had shot me… at point blank range. So why was I still awake, why was I still breathing, and why was my heart ready to beat out of my chest.

I watched as Zerro fell to his knees. Another shot sounded off and I wasn't sure what was happening. Was Zerro killing himself?

Then I heard Mack's laughter. It filled the room and made my stomach quake.

"You thought this bitch would be smart enough to do something like this?" Mack asked. He was talking to Zerro, and my eyes scanned the ground for the gun. Would I save Zerro again? After everything he had done to me just now?

Zerro was on the ground, his face filled with pain as he stared at me. The look he held said he was sorry, but he still hadn't said the words. His eyes were begging for forgiveness, speaking the words he didn't say. I needed the words. I needed to know he was sorry for his betrayal.

"It was you…" he said groaning.

"Ding. Ding. Ding. Of course, it was me. Did you think I would sit idly by while you reaped the benefits of everything I had done for you? I was tired of being treated like shit while the 'King' sat on his throne. Instead, I turned you into the FBI and made a deal with them. They let me off the hook—I give them you. Not that it matters, because they're on their way here to pick you up. As for Bree, well… that hot piece of ass is coming with me."

"No…" He groaned again trying to reach for his gun. Mack kicked it away and my hope went flat. I would never be able to reach the gun now.

"Yes," Mack mocked. "Then once we're finally alone, I'm going to fuck her every way possible."

I tried my hardest to wiggle out of the ropes, but ended up on my stomach with nowhere to go.

"Leave her alone," Zerro groaned rolling over to search the floor for another weapon.

"Ha, ha. Yeah, fuck no. She's coming with me," Mack said, gripping the ropes around my midsection.

"Zerro, run, leave," I huffed out, my voice full of anguish. The words were just barely out of my mouth when I felt Mack's dirty hand fist into my hair, pulling my face into his.

"Say another word and there's going to be a fucking bullet in your head," he growled.

"Get your fucking hands off her." Zerro was barely able to get the words out, and though I wanted to look at him, I knew I couldn't. My heart was already breaking.

"How about… Fuck. No!!" Mack mocked, and then pointed his gun off in the distance. His hold on my hair was keeping me in place once I heard the gun go off again. I couldn't stop the tears from coming.

Trying as much as I could to see through the tears, I screamed until Mack released me to grab something off the floor. Looking up from the floor, I watched as a red puddle all but started to form around Zerro. Suddenly, Mack was biting at a piece of duct tape to place over my mouth.

"I love you," I cried out right before the tape was placed against my lips. Tears continued to cascade down my cheeks as I tried to say I love you over and over again. I was certain it would be the last time I would ever see Zerro alive and if he did live, he wouldn't come to save me.

"There's no point screaming. Where you're going, they love to hear women scream. They feed off the tears you cry. Believe me when I say if you thought Zerro was a monster, you're in for a ride."

"Let fucking go of me," I mumbled against the tape wiggling as much as I could. Tears were still blocking my vision, but I felt the air whip through my hair as Mack pushed us through the front door.

"No way. You're my ticket out of all of this." He sounded gleeful, and I wanted to wipe the fucking smile I knew was on his face off.

"You won't get away with this. He'll find you, and when he does, you're as good as dead." I knew there was no pleading with this kind of man.

Picking me up as if I weighed nothing more than a feather, he opened the back of what looked like a van and sat me on the edge of the entrance so he could open the other door up. My mind skidded to a halt as I realized this might be my only chance to escape. Pulling my feet together, I bunched up my legs as much as I could and pushed back as I kicked at his face.

He stumbled back only slightly. Swear words filled the air. Trying to sit up, I pushed my legs up again to get another good kick, but it did me no good. He was bigger and stronger. His hands gripped my legs as anger showed in every muscle I could see. "You're dirty fucking bitch," he said as he tried to push me further into the van.

Fighting with all my might, I pushed back, kicking

and screaming. My words were hard to hear and my kicking did nothing but wear me out.

"Let go of me," I repeated over and over again my screams were nothing but a muffle of noise against the duct tape. Another kick to the face would hopefully get him to slow down. His hands wrapped around my legs, and his fist came down hard against my cheek. For a moment, my vision blurred as pain radiated through my face. My mind went blank as light reflected in and out. I couldn't get a grip on what was happening.

"If that doesn't keep you down, then this fucking will." His words caused my head to ache as I tried to get my wits together.

Before I could respond, I felt the prick of something in my arm, and the darkness of whatever it was he had injected me with consumed me.

The Past

Zerro

"Jared. Jared…" I screamed into the phone. I was on the verge of death. I could feel the blood seeping from every pore of my body.

"Calm down, Zerro, just breathe," Jared kept repeating to me. He wanted me to calm down and just breathe. Did he not realize I was shot three fucking times? I was bleeding to death. He was lucky I was still coherent.

"They have Bree. I fucked up. I fucked up." My voice was growing weak with every word I spoke. I should've been saving my energy. I should've been thinking about anything but her, but I couldn't get the fearful look she had in her eyes out of my mind. The look I had placed there.

"What the hell happened? What do you mean they?" Jared asked his voice harsh and panicked. Could I even tell him what had happened. I was beyond ashamed. The way I had treated her. Not to mention Mack, and the fact I had trusted him.

"Fuck…" I hissed into the phone, trying to roll into

a sitting position.

"What happened, Zerro. I just left less than twenty-four hours ago…?" Jared sounded astonished, and I didn't even care. I didn't care about explaining anything to him. All that mattered was I survived so I could kill Mack and get Bree back.

"Zerro!" Jared yelled.

"Yeah," I said weakly, I wasn't going to make it. He wasn't going to get here fast enough, and I was going to die. I was going to meet my fate at the hands of one of my most trusted men.

"Stay with me, dude, stay with me." I could hear Jared's pleading voice but couldn't force any words from my mouth. It was as if everything in my life had slowed down. Memories of my mother, father, and Bree filtered in and out. A ray of colors showed behind my eyes as if they were the moon, sky, and stars on a dark night.

"Mack…. It was Mack…" I was just able to get out before the world started to grow darker.

"Alzerro, you're not allowed to fucking die on me, do you hear me?" It sounded as if Jared was screaming through a long tube. By the time his voice reached my ears, it was muffled and had lost its effect. Instead of it sounding like he was yelling, all I heard was barely a whisper.

"Alzerro, you listen to me. You have to stay alive. You have to kill Mack. You have to get revenge…." My eyes stung as I tried to open them, and my body felt hard—as if bricks were being piled on me piece by piece, brick by brick. I knew I needed to keep my eyes open. I knew I needed to keep thinking. I needed to hold on to hope, but I couldn't when the darkness called to me.

"Zerroooo…" Those were the last words I would ever hear, and the last image to hit me in the face was one of Bree, and the look on her face knowing I had let her down. I cut her deep with my actions not even realizing the knife was in my hand. I stabbed her in the back because I thought she had betrayed me. In reality, it was I who had caused her the ultimate betrayal.

Then the darkness came and there was no point trying to fight it. It was inevitable.

Inevitable

chapter two

Zerro

My body ached badly as I threw my legs over the side of the bed. The cotton sheets felt soft against my skin—soft just like Bree's skin. I had to shake my head to get the memories to leave my mind.

"You're too weak to be getting up and moving around," Jared said interrupting my thoughts. I looked up from the hardwood floor and up to his face. His eyes were dull, reflecting no light. His face was sunken in, and it looked as if he hadn't shaved in months. I didn't have room to talk, though. I don't look much better I'm sure. It had been three weeks since I had last seen Bree, since I had last touched her. Since I had allowed Mack, the fucking snake, into my cabin. Just thinking about it caused my blood to boil.

"Funny, last I remember you didn't have a medical degree," I retorted in a smart-ass tone, adjusting myself. My leg was fucked up from the gunshot. I had lost a shit ton of blood, and though the shots I had taken to the chest hurt, nothing hurt as bad as trying to move my leg when it had stitches and pins in it.

Leaning against the door of the room, he smiled at

9

me as if he thought what I said was actually funny, when really I was just trying to be an asshole.

"You don't need a medical degree to know you should be lying in bed. Resting. Cooling off. Staying hidden." In one whole sentence, he named four things I would rather not be doing.

"No…" I hissed out as a burning sensation flowed through my leg. "I would rather not just lay here while Bree is out there and that ass fucking hole has her. I would rather do anything, but sit here and hope and pray for something good to come from all of this." I sneered.

"Hoping and praying won't do shit in this situation, but going into something without a plan won't help either. Do you want to put yourself in line for death again?" I kept my eyes trained on the floor as I attempted to stand for the first time in weeks. My body was worn and tired, but at the same time, it was begging for a release of energy. To get up and move around. Nothing Jared was saying was going to stop me from doing what needed to be done.

My foot hit the floor, and although there wasn't any weight on it yet, I was slightly hesitant to stand. It hurt like a bitch lying down, so I'm sure it would be no better standing. It didn't matter though; I had to start somewhere. Putting most of my weight on my arms, I pushed myself up slowly attempting to push the majority of my weight onto my good side. Once I was ready, I shifted weight to the other side, ever so slowly.

"I swear to fucking god, you have a death wish, Zerro. A death fucking wish," Jared muttered under his breath angrily.

"No death wish, Jared…" I hissed out between clenched teeth as a burning sensation radiated up my leg. It hurt, but not as bad as I thought it would. "I have a need for revenge. A burning, all-consuming rage to have revenge on Mack; to get Bree back. Sitting here in this fucking bed, not getting better, not moving, and allowing myself to think

10

about it more, just adds unneeded fuel to the fire."

In my rant to Jared, I didn't even realize I had come to stand on both feet while holding the side of the bed. Releasing a deep breath, I let go of the sheets and stood by myself. I looked up at Jared and watched him walk over to me—waiting for me to fall to the ground I was certain. I wasn't used to feeling weak, to needing someone. If anything, the need for help just made me angrier. I wasn't coping with the shit that went down. I was simply waiting it out until the moment I could sink my knife into Mack's flesh.

"Bree needs you, Zerro. She needs you to come and save her wherever the fuck she is, but she also needs you to be strong and healthy because, without those things, you're useless to her. If you go barreling in there without a plan, without fully being healed, you become a liability."

Fuck. Running a hand through my hair and down my face, I allowed a sigh of release. As much as I fucking didn't want to admit it, which was a lot, Jared was right. He was right, and I'd be damned if it didn't make it fucking worse.

"You're right... but Bree... she needs me..." I was struggling with my next words because I still wasn't sure about where Bree and I stood. Her father had killed my mother. I had almost killed her. Fuck. All I knew for certain, even after everything that had happened, was that I loved her, and when I found her, I would release her of the debt and give her the freedom she deserved. I would protect her for the rest of her life, even if it killed me to protect her from myself.

I was so lost in my own shit storm, I hadn't realized Jared had placed his hand on my shoulder. I turned my head glaring at his hand. I knew it was just a gesture of reassurance, but nothing would assure me she was okay—at least not until I had her in my arms.

"I know you love her. There isn't any reason for you

to have to say it out loud. Just know if you don't get yourself healthy, you will be useless to her and to me."

My eyes left his hand and went to his face. He was looking at me as a friend. Talking to me as a friend. I knew why—because we were friends. Always had been, but I didn't trust people for a reason. Trusting Mack got me into this situation. What if trusting Jared pushed me into my own grave?

"You know nothing about love or my love for her. I will get better and I will find her. I will kill Mack and her father. Then I will move on with my life, never thinking back to this very moment," I growled, so angry with myself and with Jared. It's an irrational thought because Jared has done nothing wrong.

I caught a glimpse of a smile crossing his face and had I not been in the condition I was in, I would've wiped the floor with his face. It didn't matter what all he had done for me. He was to respect me, treat me as I was.

"You're so right. I know nothing of love. Nothing about it," he said taking a couple steps back as he headed for the door. "I can tell you love will only get you so far. If you love her as much as you say you do, you will heal. There is no way Mack would kill her—you and I both know it. He took her for a reason." Jared's voice was almost reasoning with me, and I forced myself to continue to stare at the wood grain in the floor.

We were in Jared's home and everything in it represented him… I've said it before, and I'm sure I'll say it again… he was right. Gritting my teeth, I forced out the words I had never said to anyone. "Thank you… for helping me." I lifted my face, my eyes landing on a photo on the wall. It was one of him and his mother before she was killed. Just like mine.

He looked similar to her. Dark hair and eyes. Beautiful as ever. It made me wonder how he had even started working for me. He was one of the good ones, and to be caught up in this drama wasn't fair to him. I owed his family more than that.

"Zerro, get better, get the girl, and be happy. You have nothing to thank me for." He completely dismissed me and turned around to walk out of the room to leave me be. As much as I thought to be alone was the right thing, I knew it was wrong. Thoughts of Bree came to the surface, and I wondered what she was going through. How much longer could she hold on? Was she still alive? It was those thoughts that reminded me I love her. I would do whatever I could to apologize to her for my actions. I refused to allow her to think the last memories of me were of some evil monster because, though it may be true, I'm also someone else. I'm a lover... and I love her.

"How does your leg feel?" Jared asked as he set a bowl of soup in front of me. It had been a few days since I had started walking around again, and I was just getting used to moving around more and more. My muscles ached, and sometimes I felt like I might collapse, but then I would think of Bree and all she must have been going through.

"It's fine," I responded, dipping my spoon into the broth of the chicken noodle soup. It smells delicious and my stomach growled in approval. Though I was hungry, a tinge of guilt burrows itself into my mind, and I dropped the spoon into the bowl. I couldn't eat not knowing what was happening to her. It didn't matter what was said, or what had taken place. The way I treated her... There was simply no excuse. I should've known better.

"You don't have to feel guilty about eating," Jared chimed in. I couldn't force myself to look at him. I didn't want him reading my thoughts. I was supposed to be the King, the man who ran everything with an iron fist. Instead, I ran nothing. My empire had crumbled, and everything that meant the most had been stolen from me.

"It's not guilt," I lied. I was on the verge of losing my temper again. I was tired of being caged, being told what to do, and how I needed rest. What I needed was Bree. I didn't care about anything else. I would get my revenge.

"Well, that's a crock of shit." He laughed, setting his spoon down on the table. I didn't know where to go from here. There was nothing I could say to help me. I needed to take action.

"Call it whatever the fuck you want. I don't care. I needed to figure out a plan, and then I needed to implement it because I would get her back, and I would gut Mack. No one lied to me and got away with it." Simply admitting he had pulled the wool over my eyes angered me. It made me feel weak in the eyes of my people, and I wasn't weak.

"Whatever. Do what you need to," he said, frustrated with me, I was sure. I couldn't blame him, but I was tired of being caged. I was tired of being told what to do, and to that I needed to rest. My leg was better, my chest no longer hurt, and the pain was a distant memory. All that mattered was Bree. I would blaze a trail of fire across the world to find her. She was mine, and I would make it known to the world.

chapter three

Bree

"Get up you stupid bitch." I heard the voice before I could register what was happening. Cold water fell on me, dousing any further movements. I was strong, really strong, but this shit was wearing on me. They kept me in a fucking hole, thrown in here since day one. Every time they came to torment me, they wore masks as if they thought I didn't know who the fuck they were. I didn't know who they were, but I knew they worked for Mack. Mack. Just saying his name caused my blood to boil.

I had very little given to me, and I knew there was a purpose behind this. They didn't want me to get comfortable. They didn't want me to feel at home, and I didn't. Food was sent down in small rations, just enough to keep me from starving to death. Crackers, peanut butter sandwiches, and small bottles of water quickly became my only meal throughout the day.

Once in a while, if I were lucky, a bucket of water was sent down so I could clean myself. On those rare occasions, I also got a change of clothes.

These clothes were never my size and always had a distinct smell to them, which only made me feel dirty all over again. They wanted to break me with their words until I was nothing, but I refused to give them the satisfaction. At night, as I lay my head on the soiled mattress with springs poking out while wrapped up in a worn blanket, I hugged my pillow thinking of my life before all of this.

The hole was cold, a bottomless pit of nothing. It only served as a place to hold me captive from the life I once lived. From the life, I had grown to know in just a few short weeks. A life with him. My mind was an indecisive mess. I couldn't tell what day it was let alone what month. It felt as if I had been hidden here for an eternity.

"Was that really fucking necessary?" I growled unable to hold back my anger a second longer as I looked up to the only place allowing light into my darkness. The entrance to my own personal hell. I had held onto hope in the beginning when Zerro would come and save me, but after three weeks of this shit, give or take, it had slipped away. I knew if he were coming he already would have, and for some reason, the thought only stirred the fire to get out of this fucking hole that much more.

"Was it needed?" he mocked laughing down at me, his voice making me want to vomit. "Of course it was needed. Your stupid ass wouldn't wake up." I clenched my fists, digging my nails into the dirt covered ground to the point of pain. But I didn't whimper. I didn't even wince. The point of this hole was to shatter me until I no longer recognized the person I once was. Make me resilient to them. Make me break. Make me forget about my life outside of this place. What they didn't take into account was, instead of it breaking me, it built me up. It made me stronger.

"Weird, I didn't hear you say wake up. All I heard was you call me a stupid bitch. Clearly, you're the bitch, but you do know you are also the stupid fucking one as well, right?" I narrowed my eyes, locking my own with his. His mask was firmly in place, but I could tell, one day I was going to push him just enough to reveal himself.

I watched as he threw the bucket down, dirt swirling around in the air as it landed by my feet. "You're lucky the boss wants you alive; otherwise, I would've fucked that pretty pussy already. Then I would've slit your throat and watched you bleed out." Somehow, I managed not to cringe, not even a tiny bit. I didn't even care about what he was saying.

Instead, I smiled. "You're stupid because when Zerro comes for you, you'll be running for the fucking hills." I wasn't sure why I said it, as I was losing hope he would come, but I had to have something to hold onto if I wanted to get out of here alive.

"Listen up, bitch. Whenever he comes for you, which he won't, it will be to kill you. Have you forgotten you're the enemy in his eyes?" He was mocking me. His eyes promised all kinds of things, and I knew, if he ever got his hands on me, he would try something.

Instead of luring myself into a deeper conversation where he would make me feel like I was beating my head against rocks, I simply zipped my lips. Allowing what he said to bother me would just bring more self-doubt, and given the situation I was in, it would be the last thing I needed.

"Did you hear me, bitch? I said you're the enemy. Your father killed his mother. What don't you understand about that? E.N.E.M.Y. That's what you are." He spelled the words out as if I were a dumb fuck who couldn't comprehend what he was saying.

"I know how to fucking spell. I don't care if he thinks I'm the enemy, my father didn't do shit." I was astonished. After everything, I was still sticking up for my father. I mean, he wasn't here trying to figure out where his fucking daughter was.

An evil laugh left the masked man's mouth, and I narrowed my eyes at him. From this distance, I couldn't make out his height to weight ratio, and even if I could take him, I didn't have the slightest clue on how the fuck I was going to get out of this hole.

"You know nothing about your father, do you?" He wasn't really asking a question. I knew he was about to tell me something I didn't want to hear.

"I know he's my dad and that's all that matters." I had nothing more to say, so instead, I looked at my feet covered in dirt from the ground. I felt dirty, used, and abused, even though no one had touched me. Yet.

"You hear this…" I rolled my eyes. He must be talking to the other masked man who occasionally delivered shit for this nob job. "Little ole bitch here thinks her dad is the good guy in all of this." I could hear his gruff laughter even though I was trying to block it out. I need to find a way out of this mess, out of this god for-fucking-saken hole.

"Is there a chance I could possibly get a shower someday… like soon… maybe?" I goaded, completely unfazed by their need to instill fear in me. I wasn't scared of them. I knew I should've been, and there was probably something seriously fucked up in my brain for me not to be, but they hadn't done anything other than belittle me.

"A golden shower maybe?" the man joked, even though I was sure he wasn't kidding.

"No thank you, asshole…" I muttered under my breath throwing myself against the dirt covered wall. Where were we exactly? There was no way they could keep me in here forever. Someday, I would have to be released, right? Or would they keep me down her? Would they kill me? Anxiety crept up on me fast. What if I was really down here forever?

I dug my nails into the dirt as if to root myself into the wall. I would be okay. I could do this. I was strong. I knew what I was up against. My breaths were coming in and out at an outrageous pace, my chest heaving with every inhale as I sunk to the ground. My chest felt as if at any second, my lungs were going to collapse, the dirt surrounding me becoming the last thing I would ever see.

"Calm down, *Piccolo*." I heard those words every time I closed my eyes. His deep voice basked me in a river of heat. Just thinking about him caused my heart to beat erratically.

I could do this—I had to do this. Standing up, I paced the small hole. How the hell did I get down here anyway? They probably fucking threw me... wouldn't put it past them.

I needed to find a way out. I needed to do something even if it was dangerous, even if it provoked them to take action. If I didn't, I surely would die down here.

Quietness surrounded me. The only sounds heard were the chirping of the birds and my own heartbeat. Where the hell did they go? No fucking way would they walk away leaving me here.

"Hey, fuckers, let me out of here," I screamed. It wasn't useless really. Yeah, my voice might hurt, but talking would annoy the fuck out of them, and eventually, one of them would have to come down here and do something about it. Then again, maybe all the noise would get someone's attention.

"You are all a bunch of cowards. You think you are a man because you can keep me in this hole?" I continued on, my voice holding so much anger and hate, if I didn't know I was the person screaming, I would think it was someone else.

Silence loomed, and instead of it doing something to calm me, it just pushed me closer and closer to the edge of boiling.

"Answer me, cowards. I've taken on bigger fucking men than you. You're all sad excuses of the Mafia, FBI, or whatever the fuck it is you do…" I was really fucking close to kicking rocks, which was great since that's all I could fucking kick—rocks or dirt.

More silence, great. I huffed out a breath just before I heard his disgusting voice. "You are really fucking mouthy…"

He had no clue. "Come down here and say that. We'll see how mouthy I can be…" I was baiting him, and though he had the mask in place, and I could hardly make out his eyes, I knew there wasn't much of a chance he would take the bait.

"Now I understand why your dad and Alzerro wanted to get fucking rid of you." His words hit me harder than expected. I loved my dad more than anything. He was the last person alive I could run to if I needed something. I kept telling myself maybe he just screwed up and found himself in the wrong place at the wrong time. The truth of the matter though—I knew he was the problem. What I didn't know was if my father was in the FBI, and no one was giving me answers.

"My dad never wanted to get rid of me, and even if Alzerro doesn't come for me, I'm going to get out of this fucking hole, and when I do, you better be running." I knew, when faced with danger, being fearless was what I needed. If I were anything but fearless, I would grow weak, my mind would enclose on me, and the worries and doubts would eat away at anything left.

"That's great and all, but until the moment comes, do you think you could possibly keep your yap shut?" Was he seriously asking me that?

"Fuck no, I can't." I all but snarled, and then I started screaming random words, names, lyrics, you name it and it was coming from my mouth in a haze.

"Shut the fuck up!" he growled. I could hear him rustling around with something, and I truthfully hoped he was going to let me out.

20

"Nope. I think the world would love to hear my voice." I spoke loudly just to push him over the edge he was barely hanging onto.

"Fuck…" he growled. I jumped back as a ladder tumbled down the side of the hole. Was this real? Was he really giving me a way to get out?

I hesitated knowing it could be a trick, and now that I had what I wanted, what was I supposed to do… I had no weapons, and my self-defense moves looked like a toddler walking with an open cup.

Walking towards the ladder rope, I tugged on it roughly, making sure it was secured and in place.

"You coming up to show me your kick-ass moves, or are you staying in the hole?" He was giving me a choice? These fucking kidnappers or keepers were fucking dumb.

Instead of saying anything, I gently tugged on the rope again. This time to make sure it was safe. I mean, you could never be too cautious.

Small step by small step, I came to the top. The brightness of the sun consumed my eyes for a moment, black spots clouding my vision as a ball of anxiety rolled around in the pit of my stomach.

As soon as my hands touched the topsoil, I allowed a sigh to escape my lips as if I might finally be free. Free. I wanted to snort. As if I had really known what that ever felt like. It was such a dumb thought though because who knew what lie ahead. This could very well be some sick fucking trick. A game of sorts.

"She arrives…" asshole in a black mask says. His feet were mere millimeters from my hands. Fear gripped me by the throat as my mind worked through every scenario possible. What if he pushed me? I clamped my jaw closed forcing the thought away. If this fucker pushed me, I would end him. Whenever the fuck I got up. If I got up.

Gripping the topsoil and feeling the grass blades against my fingers sent a shiver down my spine. I felt as if I could finally breathe. The man stepped back allowing me to move upward on the ladder until I was almost out. Leaning forward, I pulled myself out of the hole and through the dirt and grass. As relieved as I should have felt, my muscles ached as I found myself in a compromising position on all fours. I pulled myself from my knees, getting my footing ever so slowly.

"Oh, no you don't...." Asshole smirked as his hand landed on my shoulder like a heavy weight. My knees wobbled as his hand came down hard on my shoulder to keep me in place.

"Let go of me," I said through gritted teeth. I was so over being treated like dirt. Kneeling down on his heels so we were eye level, I took in his face. Most, if not all of his olive skin was covered in clothing, except his hands and the skin surrounding his eyelids. His eyes were a deep green, and within in them were the answers to the questions I longed to know.

His lips were thin and tilted down in a frown as if something about the predicament didn't sit well with him. His other hand reached out and his thumb grazed the bottom of my chin. As if on reflex, I flinched away, turning my head away from him.

"I know why he wanted you... Your defiance can be smelled from miles away." His breath is cool against my face, and I wanted to turn and spit right into it. My emotions were all over the place, but one thing was still true—I was mad as all fucking hell.

"I'm not defiant, asshole. I'm just not one for being held in a hole in the ground, having buckets of water thrown on me, and being talked down to like a fucking dog. Defiance isn't even the word... to describe how you make me feel." I was seething.

I watched as the side of his lips lifted into a half

smile, as if what I was saying made him happy. It would. It would make him happy to see someone like me in this situation.

Within a blink of my eye, he was standing again, his voice raised as he laughed at me. Confusion settled into my bones. What the hell was he doing?

"I make you feel something? That's hilarious." I listened to him talk while coming to a stand as slow as possible. Could I make a run for it? No. They would shoot me.

"Do you even know why you're here?" Asshole asked again as if I was actually listening to him. Since Zerro, I stared danger right in the eyes and laughed— something I could always thank him for, I guess.

"I think we went over this already, but let me tell you why I think I'm here." I pause a moment surveying the land. There was a clearing with trees on all sides and we were deep in the woods. My breaths came in as pants as my eyes caught on an old rotting stump off in the distance.

"You were saying..." He mocked his eyes glittered with amusement, and though I could see he found something funny, there was a darker secret being kept in his eyes.

"You know something..." I growled, not even caring if my accusation got me thrown back in the hole. Crossing his arms over his chest, he looked down at me.

"And you know nothing..."

"Tell me." I refused to allow him to taunt me. I need answers if he knows what happened to Zerro, and he knows what happened to my father then he's more useful than I ever thought.

"Tell you what? That Zerro is dead and your father is hiding you in a hole near your own home?" My eyes grew big, and my heart raced as I took a step back. Did he say Zerro was dead? Wouldn't I know? Wouldn't I have felt something? But that wasn't what shocked me the most. Oh, no. What shocked me most was the fact he said my father was hiding me.

"It's shocking to see someone pulled from your life, isn't it? Shocking to know your dear ole daddy isn't the person you thought he was." I don't even notice the tear that escapes my eye. One single tear. One single fucking tear defines my life.

"He wasn't pulled from my life. You know nothing about him as a person. As for my dad... he would never." The words slipped from my mouth with ease as if I was meant to say them. Zerro had been an evil man, killing countless people. People who may or may not have deserved to die.

He was dark, cruel, and sometimes I hated him.... but something inside of me loved him, too. Then there was my dad. The only person I had left, the only man who would always love me.

Could he be capable of the accusations everyone seemed to want to accuse him of? Something inside me told me he was still the same person who held me every night as I cried because I had lost my mother. Something inside of me wouldn't fully allow me to believe he would do such things.

Asshole smirked, his body eating up what little space separating us. He was a foot's distance away from me once he spoke.

"I know he has more blood on his hands than anyone I know. I know he's vindictive and willing to do anything in his power to seek revenge. I know, no matter what you think or want to believe, he isn't coming for you. I know he doesn't love you and it was all a game—"

"Stop." I could barely get the one word out as a cascading waterfall of tears fell from my eyes. I was strong until the moment he told me my dad didn't want me anymore until I heard the words come from his mouth.

"Why? Because you know it's true, and it might

actually pull you from whatever delusional place you are in your head?"

"Stop. You know nothing!" I yelled, reaching out to push him away with my hands.

"I do know something…" he barely whispered as he gripped my wrists stopping my attack on him.

"I know I was given direct orders to let you rot in this hole. To let you die." What he said hits me straight in the chest as if someone had just knocked the wind out of me and my mind begins to reel. Would my father really put me in a hole to die? Would he allow others to torment me and treat me like shit?

"Liar," I said between clenched teeth and with narrowed eyes.

"You know I'm not lying. You know this is your property. You know your father put you here... and now I'm letting you go."

"Letting me go?" I whisper, taking a couple steps back. He was letting me go? This must me a joke. He would never let me go. Would he?

"Yes. Letting you go, but first, you have to do something for me." If he couldn't tell I was shocked, there was something wrong with him.

"I'm not doing anything for you." My voice squeaked with anxiety.

"Yes, you are…" he yelled, his hands biting into my shoulders

"Get your fucking hands off of me," I yelled.

"Hit me," he growled.

"What? No." Was this guy on crack? His eyes looked fine and other than he had a part in kidnapping me, and in holding me against my will, he seemed, well… normal.

He smirked, and the look alone caused my belly to roll. "I bet I could get you to hit me… All I would have to do is slide my hand between those pretty little…"

"STOP! Leave me alone," I cried, taking a step away from him. I couldn't tell if he was being serious or baiting me.

"Make me…" His voice held a darkness I wanted to run from. The green of his eyes grew darker in that one single moment. My eyes slid over his body landing on his feet as I watched him advance on me. Every step he took, I matched with a step back.

"Just let me go. I'll run as fast as I can and you can tell them whatever you want," I cried, real fear burrowing into my mind.

"Your dad is a fucking monster just like the man you claim to love. Neither one of them wants you anymore. I mean, seriously—if they did, don't you think they would have come for you already? You are nothing more than a fucking bargaining piece to them. They used you! Used you to bring the other one down... and after I see how sweet that cunt of yours is, you are dead."

He was lying. Wasn't he?

"Stop lying to me," I screamed as I pulled my hair, fighting myself for the last bit of sanity I had left. Before I could convince myself this was a part of his game, I whipped my hand out and slapped him across his face. The instant burn soothed the raging storm inside of me as I watched a smirk come across his face.

"That's it, darling. Get mad, get fucking angry," he spewed at me right before he stretched his arms out as if he were the king of the fucking world.

"Look around, take a good look. It's not a lie. All the proof you need is in front of you, behind you. It's surrounding you, for fuck's sake, if you would only open your eyes," he whispered his breath against my cheek. He was lying. He had to be. What did he know?

"How do I know? Oh, I know everything." He answered my question as if he could read my mind.

"Stop. Just stop. I'll do whatever you want…" I

held my hands out stopping any further assault by him. His hard chest brushed against my fingers. The warmth of his skin against mine sparked something in me.

"If I threw you on the ground right now and fucked the daylights out of you, what would you do? Would you scream?" He joked with a small laugh leaving his lips. "Better yet, I bet you would love it… You would love my cock."

My already clenched fist reached out slamming into the side of his jaw. My skin stung with the connection, but I wasn't sure if I did any good since he was still standing there and looked about ten times more pissed off.

"Kick me…" he gritted out. It was then I knew he had baited me. He wanted to get a rouse out of me. Giving him a you're-fucking-crazy-and-you-know-it look, I pulled back and kicked him right in the shin. Then I did it again for good measure…

"Fuck…" I heard him mutter under his breath as he grabbed at his leg.

"Now run…" Run? He wanted me to run away? What if they found me?

"But…"

"No buts, fucking run. Run until you get to the house. Tell Zerro he owes me one." He winked at me as he lay on the ground as if I had actually kicked his ass. Inside, I smiled, but deep in the bottom of my belly, a snake of anxiety slithered its way through me. If he allowed me to go, what awaited me once I got to the house? I didn't know, but I was about to find out. I took off in a dead run toward the stump. I would find out what my father's intentions were all along. And that was my final thought as I forced myself to pick up the pace knowing the enemy could be on my heels at any second. The harshness of the air I was taking in almost broke me, but I wouldn't stop running. No. I couldn't stop running—not when my life depended on it.

Inevitable

chapter four

Zerro

My body was begging for me to kill someone, something, anything. I wanted revenge, but more than that, I wanted answers. I wanted to know what the fuck happened. Why Mack had betrayed me, where Bree was, and if her father actually killed my mom.

The only way I knew how to get these answers would end up taking me back down a long road to where it all started. John's house. Bree's childhood home. As I parked the SUV at the end of the driveway, I looked down the long dirt road. I had asked myself this question a number of times. Would I really be able to kill him? I mean, it wasn't really a question of whether I would kill him or not. More so, would Bree forgive me if she were still alive? The very fact I was even thinking about it bothering her told me she had weaseled her way deep into my skin.

I had tried—fuck, had I tried. I had done everything in my control to force her out, to make sure she was never brought into this shit. Try as I may, I knew, at the end of all of this, it wouldn't be love that conquered all. No, it would be death. I may love her, but if her father killed my mother, it made us enemies. No amount of love could make up for the hate surging through me.

The dust picked up around my feet as I walked up the long driveway. My mind wandered aimlessly about all the things it shouldn't be. Like how many times Bree had walked down this same road as a child. She had run and skipped or simply walked with her head held high.

In no time at all, my mind was coming back to the present as I came around the bend and had my first glimpse of the dilapidated farm house. It needed work, like serious work. The gutters looked as if they hadn't been cleaned in months, and the shutters were falling from the windows. The once white paint of the house had peeled away and made the house look like a grayish speck.

If he was a farmer, why did his house look like this? Why did all of this seem ridiculous? Unless he wasn't a farmer, he wasn't this poor old man he made himself out to be, but instead, maybe he was working for the FBI. My mind whirled as I grew closer to the house.

There was one single truck parked in the driveway. It was his. I knew from the rust liable to fall off if you breathed on it the wrong way. I knew it was his because I knew the people who owed me money.

Slowly, I walked up and around the truck, my hand on my gun. I wasn't concerned with killing someone. No, I knew someone was going to die.

Walking around the house slowly, I crept up the front steps of the porch. I knew the fucker was here and was probably sitting in this house, watching and waiting.

The boards underneath my feet creaked with every step I took, giving away my presence. Why I cared, I wasn't sure. Even as the King of a Mafia crumbling around me, I felt I still needed—no, wanted the element of surprise.

"I knew you would come." His voice was raspy, and cigar smoke filled my nostrils. I wasn't even inside the door yet and my gun was drawn. I wouldn't have been surprised if I had put the bullet in his head that second and walked away. Small talk wasn't my thing.

Stepping over the threshold, I took in the house again. It looked very much the same and the mystery of who John was grew deeper and deeper. How could someone like him allow his daughter to live in these conditions?

"If you knew I was coming, then you should've prepared yourself." My voice was full and angry. Not just because of my feelings toward him—for something he may or may not have done, but because of the situation he had brought Bree into. He was reckless, careless, and it was a fucking load coming from someone like me, but even I knew it.

"Prepared for what exactly?" he retorted, smirking at me as he blew a puff of smoke out. I stood just before the entrance to the living room. He was dressed in a suit and was sitting casually as ever. Long gone was the poor, helpless farmer. Fuck, I should just kill him right now—after all, this was all just a ploy.

"You're dressed for the occasion now, aren't you?" I mocked back. I wasn't fucking stupid. I had no one behind me anymore. Everyone had crumbled, fallen, or fled in the end.

His eyes grew large as he set the cigar down on an ashtray. This man was the father of the woman I loved and was the only reason he was still standing and not dead at my feet.

"You know then, don't you? You know I took your mom's pathetic fucking life well, she hid you from us." He laughed and it caused my insides to quake with anger. My finger was getting really fucking trigger happy.

"Cut the shit. I know you fucking did it, but what I don't know is why. What I don't get is who you work for, and if I don't get the answers I want, I'll put a bullet in every single person's head until I do get an answer," I spat at him. My gun was aimed and ready. I didn't even give a shit anymore. I would take the world down in a burning blaze if I had to in order to find the answers.

He shifted in his seat before standing. His eyes showed nothing but hate and anger. Not an ounce of remorse could be found, and for a smidge of a second, I wondered if this would be what I looked like the moment before I put a bullet in someone's head. Shaking my head, I pushed the thought away—I wasn't a monster. I wasn't a ruthless killer. When I killed, it was because the person deserved it—and I knew my mother didn't deserve to die.

Laughing, he said, "You'll kill everyone? Every single person who may or may not have an answer? What about my daughter? She has answers. She knows shit, but yet you still wanted between her legs. Was it good?" He was a sick fucker, and when he finally had his chance at death, I would make sure it was painful.

Narrowing my eyes, I glared at him. "Bree has nothing to do with this." I forced out the lie easily. She had everything to do with this. If it came down to it, if it came down to her or me, I wasn't sure I could save myself. I wasn't sure I could save either of us.

"Oh, but she does. She has every fucking thing to do with it." My anger was building the more and more we talked. I hadn't come here for this.

"I don't give a shit about Bree. I give a shit about answers, and I won't be leaving here without them."

A loud gasp sounded behind me, and I held my breath for a moment before turning around. My eyes landed on her dirt covered body, and I almost lowered my gun. The urge to go to her and see if she was okay was slowly taking over. I had to keep up this facade or he would see how much of a weakness she was for me. I continued to aim at John's head as I took in her appearance. The condition she was in was enough to make me pull the fucking trigger and put a bullet in his head. Her hair was matted, dirt was caked on her face, and her clothes were a mess. She looked as if she had been held up in a dirt pile.

"What the fuck?" I heard as John mumbled under his breath. "Bree, what are you doing here?" He was just as surprised to see her as I was. Hell, I planned to find her after all of this, but from the way her father was acting, I had to assume he knew where she was all along.

"What am I doing? Why the fuck did you put me in a hole in the fucking field? Why the hell—" She stopped mid-sentence, unable to finish her sentence.

"Bree." Her father scolded her like a child. I was getting the feeling he hadn't been truthfully honest with her yet.

"You lied to me. You put me in a fucking hole, and you lied to me. Do you work for someone?" Deep betrayal could be heard in her voice as the words flowed freely from her lips.

Rolling his eyes, he smiled. "I was protecting you, child. Simple as it is, I knew you wouldn't stay away from him." He was referring to me now as *him*, huh?

"You fucking lied," she mumbled again as if in disbelief.

A moment passed as her eyes began to look glassy. I turned to face John again, and I managed to catch the smirk on his face. He wanted to use her against me. He wanted to hurt me. Fuck, he even wanted to hurt his own daughter. Fuck him. I would use the one thing I knew had to mean the most to him. He might not have a problem hurting her feelings, but he definitely didn't want her dead.

I was going to regret this more than anything in my life. I was certain it would hurt me more than her, but I needed leverage. Turning around fast, I reached out, gripping her by the arm. She tripped coming out of her trance as I pulled her body in front of mine. I placed the barrel of the gun at her temple and waited for him to say something.

I could practically hear Bree's heart beating out of her chest. Was she afraid? Did she think I would actually be able to do this? Did I?

Looking past her shoulder, I caught site of John with a huge smile on his face.

"You actually expect me to think you would kill her? I know how you treated her while she was staying with you. You barely laid a hand on her. Now you're threatening me with this?"

Fuck. Sweat formed on my brow. I was about to be fucking out of something to use if I didn't do something fast.

"I do," I said as an idea hit me. Pulling the gun away from Bree's head, I slipped it into the back of my pants, and I swear I could hear her sigh with relief. Little did she know things were about to get ten times crazier. I just hoped she would be able to hang on a little longer.

"Zerro, we don't have to," she whimpered. She was scared and she had reason to be. If her father didn't cooperate with me, I would have to hurt her.

Getting a good grip on the knife, I watched John's eyes grow bigger than ever as I turned Bree around in my hold, gripped her by the throat, and slammed her back into the wall. My knife at the side of her neck meant business.

"Now tell me what it is I want to hear," I growled, ignoring the terror in Bree's eyes. I had to do this. I had to.

"You won't…" John joked with a laugh stuck in his throat.

"I will," I retorted as I gripped the knife and pushed it softly into Bree's crème white skin. I could feel her pulse jumping underneath my fingers. I could smell her fear, and I had no way of telling her it would be okay.

"Kill her then."

"Okay," I responded, shrugging my shoulders. Gazing up into her terror-filled eyes, I pushed the knife into her skin harder—praying to fucking God he was goading me. Her small hand reached up to push my hand away, but instead of stopping, I pressed the knife further into her skin. A small trickle of blood escaped and slid down her neck. I sent her a warning glare, reminding her of all I was capable of doing.

"Stop!" she cried out. I was waiting for the tears I saw in her eyes to fall, but they never did. Her breaths were now pants, and I watched as she tried to swallow past the fear lodged in her throat. Everything was in slow motion, and for one fucking second in my life, I didn't want to kill someone. I didn't want to shut out the light in someone else's life.

"Okay… Okay…" I heard John's pleas, and immediately, pulled the blade away, my eyes skimming over the cut before turning back to John.

"Are we on the same page now, or do I need to do something else? When I said I took her as a form of payment, I meant I was taking her pussy to fuck it until it was useless. I didn't say I was going to grow attached to it. I definitely didn't say I would keep her the fuck alive." The words coming from my mouth made me cringe so I couldn't imagine what was going through Bree's mind.

"Killing her won't get you the answers you want." I had underestimated John. I had figured he didn't care about Bree, and I was wrong. Whatever he was doing with her was out of protection.

"Killing her will make you see what it's like to lose your last living relative. It will make you *relate*." I didn't even recognize my own voice, and I felt the person I had newly become slipping away. I couldn't bear to look Bree in the eyes… not yet. Releasing my hold on her throat, I watched as she sank to the floor with exhaustion and shock evident in her features. *Come the fuck on. Stay with me, Bree…*

"What do you want to know?" John asked, going

from standing to sitting as if he couldn't handle what was taking place right before his eyes. The blade in my hand was heavy as guilt pressed hard down on my chest. How could I have been so conflicted in that very moment? This was the moment I had waited for my entire life.

"I think we both know the answer to that question. I want answers, I want to know who killed my mother, and I don't want to go in a fucking circle trying to get them." My voice was animalistic as my eyes bled into John's eyes. I could practically see the beads of sweat forming on his face.

That's right, fucker. I have your one and only weakness in my grasp.

"Dad, just tell him you didn't do it." Bree's voice croaked as she spoke. John's gaze slid from mine to hers, and then back to mine again. I didn't have time for this, nor did I have the patience.

Bending down, I gripped her by the arm pulling her up to her feet. She was weak and didn't even resist my touch. Had she lost hope?

"Things are about to get really fucking bloody if you don't tell me what I want to fucking hear."

His meaty hand rubbed over his bald head and then down his face as worry formed in his eyes.

"I killed her. I killed your mom. My partner and I were working for the FBI at the time, and I killed her. It's not like we fucking wanted to kill her." I heard his words, but at the same time, I didn't. My body felt as if it were floating as if it was far, far away. Something in my mind clicked and I released my hold on Bree.

"You didn't want to?" I rambled, wanting nothing more than to put the bullet in his head right that second.

"Your family had killed tons of our men. Our job was to go in and snuff you out. We needed to put an end to the family. Your mother wouldn't help us, and it left her as a loose string in the mix of things. You know what they say about lose…" I didn't even give him a moment of time before I jumped on him. My fist went flying into his jaw and I saw red. My mother was not a loose string.

"A loose string? A loose string to what? You trying to kill people who did nothing wrong?" I was screaming now, my rage mounting with every hit to his face.

Turning his face to me, he smiled. His white teeth showed through the mess of blood. It was in his smile I found the need to finish the job. He deserved to die. A death for a death.

Suddenly, it was as if everything went in slow motion. I could hear Bree's screams as I reached into my pocket and pulled out the gun. His eyes grew wide with fear as he tried to pull away, but there was no hope for him. Placing the barrel against his forehead, I pulled the trigger. No remorse shattered within me, not even as I watched his brains splatter on the floor behind him, or the fact I had just killed the father of the woman I loved…

Instead, I sat there above him, watching the life leave his body. Bree's cries turned to lunatic screams as she scrambled across the floor. Her small hands pawed at his shirt as she pleaded with him to wake up, to be alive. But even I knew there wasn't any hope in what she was doing. He had to die, even if it killed me. Even if it killed me to hurt her—nothing spoke louder to me than my need for blood.

"Daddy…." I heard her cry, tears streaking through the dirt on her face, and I didn't even care. I didn't care about anything.

"Get up," I said sternly. Her head shook, and I knew something bad was about to happen. I knew I was about to break, to hurt her, again.

"How the fuck could you do this?" She turned to me, angry and sad. I learned long ago showing emotions like she was made us weak. I understood I had just shot and killed her father, but this was life. When you messed with my people, took people from me, then I was forced to do something about it.

"A life for a life. We're even. Now get up and let's fucking leave before his goonies come up here." I didn't have to be told he had other men working with him. I knew it. I was smart in that aspect.

She shuffled to her feet, tears still falling from her eyes. "You think I'm going to fucking go anywhere with you? Leave me the fuck alone. I should call the cops on you right now."

I almost laughed as I watched her gaze swing around the room as if she were looking for something. When did she become so strong? "Not a good idea, *Piccolo*," I warned, pointing the gun at her. Were we enemies now? Would I have to kill her, too?

"Do it. Shoot me. I bet you can't. I bet you're too big of a fucking coward. God knows, I know it. My father knew it, too. That's why he killed your mother…" I had seen red before she finished speaking.

My hand reached out and gripped tightly onto the hair on her scalp as I pulled her face into mine. My nostrils were flaring, and my blood was burning. I was conflicted. I wanted to kick her ass, but at the same time, I just wanted to drag her the fuck away from all of this. There was no fear in her eyes—just red-hot anger.

"Never. Ever. Fucking talk to me like that again. You're going with me, and you will do whatever the fuck I tell you."

Instead of releasing her, I stared deeply into her eyes, not even noticing the way her face soured. As if out of nowhere, I watched her pull back and spit on me. My chest heaved, and my anger spiraled out of control.

Releasing my grip on her hair, I wrapped one hand around her throat, and the other along her jaw.

"I was kind to you, I understood you, and I cared for you. I still fucking do, but you knew if I found out, it would be his dead body on the ground. You're lucky it's not yours." Did I really mean it?

Clenching her teeth with deep anger as she tried to pull away, she seethed, "I would much rather be dead than to have to fucking go anywhere with you." She could be mad all she wanted. Her ass was still stuck with me. She had nowhere else to go, and I had already grown too attached to her to allow her to go.

"Then I'll be sure to make it your own personal hell." My fingers dug harder into her cheeks, and I knew there would be bruises if I didn't stop, but I didn't care. I didn't care about anything,—her hurting, the fact I had killed her father—nothing mattered.

"It already is," she ground out. As I stared deeply into her eyes, I watched the pain and anger swirl. I had caused her this heartache— even if I didn't want to know if this would make or break us.

Instead of responding to her, I released her face with a defaming look. I had taken the beautiful, innocent angel she was and had molded her into the devil's toy. I had broken her beyond repair. Gripping her arm tight, I pulled her toward the door, only to be stopped. She was digging her feet into the ground, and I knew if I didn't do something fast, we would be caught. There was no time to sit around and wait for everyone else to get here.

"Fine, then," I growled. Taking a step toward her, I gripped her by the hips, picked her up, and threw her over my shoulder.

"Put me the fuck down," was her first response. Though I ignored her foul mouth, I couldn't ignore the pounding and scratches on my back. I knew she wanted me to react, but if she thought she was going to get a rise out of me, she was wrong. If anything, it made me want to nail her ass against a tree.

"You're going to get us killed with your fucking screaming, yelling, and nonsense thinking," I said continuing down the driveway. I could hear her huffs, anger radiating out of her like an overheated furnace.

"Getting us killed? Are you fucking crazy? No, wait. You are! You just killed my dad at point blank range. My dad…" Her voice cut off, and I could tell she was on the verge of tears. Maybe she didn't want to think her dad was capable of such venomous acts or she didn't want to face the music—either way, she had to know it would come down to this.

"Yeah. You will get us killed if you keep your fucking yap open. While I know I just killed your father, shut your fucking mouth. Mourn it later. Learn to deal with it. I never said I was a good man, Bree. I told you I was out for vengeance. Love wasn't going to stop me from seeking it. Be mad, hate me, cuss me out, and never want to see me again, but know you can never run from me."

Silence settled over us as her chest heaved against my shoulders. For the first time in my life, I had met someone who I didn't want to hurt, who I had wanted to take the pain from. Even though I wanted all those things, I was bred to kill, to hate, and to make those suffer who had made me suffer. A death for a death made us even. Bree would have to learn the hard way, though my love for her was deep, my need for vengeance was the same.

Bree

My chest heaved as I held in the tears I desperately wanted to release. Zerro had ripped the last living person from my life. He had shot and killed him in cold blood. It didn't matter if I had loved him—nothing mattered because he had killed my father.

He placed me on the cold leather seat of the SUV and shut the door, not saying a word. I should open the door, I should run though I knew it would be useless. He would just hunt me down and haul me back here. As I sunk further into the seat, my mind sunk further into the abyss. How could he do something so cruel? How could he kill someone and feel no remorse? John was my father—it didn't matter to me what he had done. None of it did. What mattered was he was dead, and I had no one. Nothing. I was just like him. Just like Alzerro King.

"You'll move on," he whispered to no one. It had to be no one because I wasn't listening to a fucking word he said. The second I got the chance, I would leave. I would run. I would escape his hold. There was now no doubt in my mind he was a living, breathing monster—far worse than the ones you heard about in fairytales.

"I hate you." I spat the words at him, hoping they would hit him with the intensity of my fist.

"Get in fucking line," he spat back at me without remorse in his words.

"He was everything to me. He was my father. My fucking father. You killed the last living member of my family—for revenge? Do you feel better? Does hurting me make your heart red again?" I screamed these words across the center console, tears streaming down my face so heavily I couldn't see anything. There was a fist-sized hole punched through my chest by the very man I loved.

Eventually the car settled into silence, but I refused to shut up. I refused to be anything but angry and sad. I was hurting. I was breaking and it was his fault. All his fucking fault.

Wiping away the tears so I could see the face of the monster, I stared into a pair of warm honey-colored eyes. "When I look at you, I see a small boy out on a mission to bring the world to its knees. To take anyone and everything out—anything undeserving of your attention. But maybe, just fucking maybe, it's you who's undeserving of the rest of us. Maybe it's you who needs to take a look around and realize the world owes you nothing. And killing people like my father gets you nothing. It doesn't make you feel better. It causes you to lose the most important person in the world to you—*me*."

I watched as his knuckles gripped the steering wheel with strength I had never seen before. Was he going to kill me next, too? Would it even matter? I wasn't sure I would care at this point.

"This is the life of the Mafia, Bree. This is what happens when someone betrays someone. You knew I was on the hunt for someone. You knew if I found him, I would kill him. It just so happened to be bad luck it turned out to be your father."

My eyes felt as if they were about to roll out of my head as I listened to him. He wasn't even sorry. It sounded more like a *I'm-sorry-I-Killed-Your-Dad-But-It-Had-To-Happen* thing.

"Do you hear yourself?"

"Do you?" he screamed back, his face growing red with anger.

"Let me go."

"Fuck you, Bree," he growled, ignoring my comment as he turned the car on, threw it into reverse, and pulled out of my driveway. We hadn't even talked about what had happened to him, to me. Hours ago, I would've been glad to know he was alive and wanted to save me, but now—now I wanted to be the one to put the bullet in his head and bury him six feet under.

"I will never love you again. You're the dirt beneath my feet," I whispered my voice dark and unsettling.

For a moment, I didn't think he heard me, but then a sigh escaped his lips. I directed my attention to the road while I allowed the tears desperately wanting to fall to build inside of me. I would rather drown myself than look weak in the face of someone like him.

"The funny thing about it is you love me anyway." I could practically see the smile on his face, and it made me sick. It made my insides twist into a hateful rush of anger.

Seething, I refused to say anything else, allowing myself to think more about my father. I wasn't even given a chance to say goodbye. My heart ached. How could I move on from this?

Pushing myself further into my seat, I heard Zerro's phone ring. My mind wondered who it could be. Had he already called someone to bury my father?

"What?" Zerro growled his face contorted in anger as he switched his hands on the steering wheel so he could talk and drive. I could hear the person on the other end yelling.

"I told you I was going out," Zerro mumbled focusing on the road and ignoring me. More talking on the other end and then a loud sigh filled the car. "Yeah, because I already killed him. I have her in the car with me."

Turning, I narrowed my eyes at him. Who else had known about this plan? Were there more people? There were a lot of questions unanswered. I really wish I could've asked my dad why he did it. Why he caused this big huge blowout. I wish Zerro would've let him talk.

"What the fuck?"

I listened as intently as I could and watched Zerro's face go white as a sheet. Whatever was being said on the other end wasn't something I wanted to hear I was sure. I had suffered enough heartache for the day. For a lifetime.

More talking on the other end and my mind began to wonder. What could be going on? Zerro's eyes looked worried, and from a single look, I knew whatever was being said would shake the already unstable ground we were standing on.

"Yeah... Yeah... We'll talk about it when we get there," Zerro said hanging up the phone before the person on the other end could say something else.

"Who was that?" I couldn't stop myself from asking.

"Jared." Rolling my eyes, I should've known. I should've known he would be the first person to go to after all of this.

"What did he say?"

One hand gripped the steering wheel while the other ran through his dark hair, pulling on it as if to relieve some tension. His eyes captured mine in a hold so intense shivers ran down my spine. I loathed him, but at the same time, my heart tugged toward him. I hated him for doing what he had done... I wanted to forget... I wanted my life to be normal.

"He found out something. And it's about to change

both of our lives." Balling my hands into fists, I narrowed my eyes at him. He had already done something that had changed both our lives forever. It was doubtful there was anything to make it worse.

"What might that be, *Alzerro*, because as of right now, nothing can make what you have done worse than what it is." My jaw ached as I clenched it. I wanted to lash out. I was so angry, so sad. I wanted to hate with everything in me.

The muscles along his jaw ticked with anger as he kept his eyes on the road ignoring my hateful comment. When he didn't answer me right away, it only managed to add fuel to the burning fire.

"Huh? Tell me, Alzerro, because right now, there isn't much more that can fucking go wrong. I'm homeless, parentless, and I don't have a fucking dime to my name. Every fucking thing has been ripped from me." Every word I said flew from my lips with ease as if they had been sitting at the entrance for some time waiting to be unleashed.

Turning his face to mine, he looked at me and then back to the road before speaking.

"I'm sorry all this misfortune has happened to you, Bree." His eyes looked sad, but there was nothing else able to give way to a bleeding heart. He wasn't sorry, and he didn't care.

"Right," I mocked turning my body and mind away from him. The trees and open fields would be better company to me than the manipulating monster sitting beside me.

As the miles passed, and the silence consumed us, my mind kept drifting back to my father. I closed my eyes just for a moment to relive his smile and simple touch. My father might have killed Alzerro's mother, and even if I didn't agree with it, I knew there had to be a reason. Unlike Alzerro, I knew it wouldn't be something good. If my father worked for the FBI, there had to be a reason. It was hard enough to imagine him as someone who killed others.

Minutes passed; just as my exhausted mind began to shut down, and my eyes began to close, we pulled onto another road, and minutes later into a driveway. The house was a simple cookie cutter style looking similar to everyone else's on the block. It definitely wasn't Mafia style. Refusing to look at Alzerro, I undid my seatbelt and opened the door and hopped out. There were no other cars in the driveway, and I wondered why.

The front door opened as my eyes roamed the front of the house. Alzerro was left standing in front of the car waiting for me. The look on his face told me he was over dealing with me. Which was fine—I was over dealing with his killing sprees, his attitude and him, in general.

"No need to babysit me, asshole," I said under my breath as I walked passed him completely ignoring his extended hand. The last thing I wanted from him was affection. I heard his intake of deep breath and his heavy steps behind my own.

"Welcome." Jared's voice met my ears, and I looked up to his face. Was this his house? What the hell were we doing here? Was this our new hideout?

Instead of saying something bitchy, I simply kept my mouth shut as I walked passed him and into what I assumed was his house. It smelled like a man and looked, well… like a bachelor pad. The walls were painted a deep gray. He had leather couches and a huge flat screen with various electronics in front of it. As I rounded the corner coming to stand in the living room, I took in the kitchen. It was simple but sleek. All black appliances lined the far wall, and it was then I started to wonder what made Jared and Zerro so different?

"I think you should sit down, Bree," Zerro said behind me, his hand landing on my shoulder heavily. I looked down at it before bringing my gaze to meet his. His hand had brought me immense pleasure, but with it had come pain. Dark, stab yourself in the heart, pain. Such deep and angry pain, I wasn't sure I would ever be able to come back from it. I had saved myself from the hole, not with an ounce of help from this man—he had killed my father and yet, he still felt he had the right to protect me? To tell me what to do. He had lost those rights a long time ago.

"I think you should remove your hand from my shoulder," I growled, taking a step back so his hand slipped from my shirt. In his eyes, a fiery rage stirred like a volcano ready to blow.

"Bree…" I turned my attention to Jared, who had concern etched into his features. His dark hair was a mess, and his eyes looked haunted as if he had been worrying over something. I knew something was going on. I guess there wasn't any better time to tell me than now.

"Tell me. Someone needs to tell me what the fuck is going on," I demanded. Gone was the broken woman I was minutes before.

Both Zerro and Jared looked at each other, worried expressions matched one another's.

"I think we should—" Jared tried to say, but I interrupted.

"I think you should tell me." My eyes narrowed at the two of them. Keeping secrets in the situation we were in wasn't good for any of us.

Zerro's large hand curled into his hair as he went around the couch to sit down.

Taking a deep breath, Jared exhaled. "John isn't your father."

The words hit me like a brick wall, and suddenly, my mind was spiraling out of control. He was lying?

"You're right because he's nothing but a dead body on my childhood home's wood floor."

Jared cringed at the words I had expelled from my mouth.

"No, I mean John never was your father." There was no real emotion behind what he said, and I took a hesitating step back. These people were trying to control me. They were making up lies. Zerro just didn't want me to tell someone.

"You're lying," I cried out, not wanting to hear anything else he had to say.

Jared shook his head, dark locks falling onto his forehead. "My father is your father. We're half-siblings. When I was digging for some info—"

"Stop," I cried out as I backed up further until I was against a wall.

"I had to help Zerro find you. I went to my father and asked if he could help. I knew nothing, Bree. I swear—"

"Just stop. Make it stop," I screamed, my throat aching. I couldn't handle this. My fingers gripped at my scalp to bring something else to life. To make me feel something other than the pain of betrayal and death.

"Bree, we're half siblings. John lied. He wasn't your father."

"I don't fucking care… I don't care…" I repeated over and over again as I slumped to the floor.

"Let me take care of her and get her cleaned up. Then you can talk to her," I heard Zerro say to Jared. I was over everything. I wanted to turn it all off. I wanted to hate and for the anger and sadness to go away. I wanted to turn it off. Having no heart meant there was no chance it could be broken.

Jared nodded dismissing Zerro. Looking up at him with tears, I could see the resemblance. Our noses were the same, our eyes held the same warm brown, and his lips were shaped the same as mine. Even though the proof was right in front of me, and there was absolutely no way to deny it, I still would. I couldn't believe it. Not now, not ever. Zerro bent down and scooped me up in his arms. I didn't want to be held or touched by the man who has caused me so much heartache, but I didn't think I could manage to walk—hell, even stand.

He carried me down the hall to the right and then into a bedroom. Sitting me on the bed, he turned around and closed the door. The silence ate away at everything that made us who we were.

Pulling at my shoes, pants, and shirt, I ripped them off. I didn't want to be covered in dirt. I didn't want to be reminded of this day ever again. I could feel the tears coming again, but refused to allow them to escape.

Once in my bra and panties, I crossed the room to what I assumed was the bathroom.

"You can't run from this." He sounded as if he had a fire in his voice. Was he angry? He had no reason to be angry.

"I can and will do whatever the fuck I want, Mr. King. You lost the right to say or do anything to me the moment you betrayed me." Once in the bathroom I slammed the door and locked it. I didn't want to see his face. I wanted nothing to do with him. My heart ached with every beat as if it were going to burst from an overflow of heartache.

I pulled away from the door just as the pounding started. I knew if he truthfully wanted in this room, he could get in.

"Leave. Go away. I hate you," I screamed placing my hands over my ears to rid myself of the noise.

"Bree, stop being childish." I could hear the terror in his voice. He thought he was losing me. Good. He needed to. He needed to know I was out of his grasps.

"GO. AWAY," I screamed again, standing to turn the shower on. I allowed the water to run making the bathroom fill with steam.

"I'll leave you alone for right now, but later, we need to talk." He sounded so full of himself. He didn't know me—not like I thought anyway. Ignoring him, I slipped into the hot stream of water. I arched into the water—God, how long had it been since I had a decent wipe down since I had actually been clean?

"My life…" I cried. Though the hot water was pouring down over me, my tears still stained my cheeks. John wasn't my father…. I sunk to the bottom of the tub, my heart and mind aching as I placed my hand on my chest. I could feel the chain beneath my fingertips and the weight of the heart dangling against my chest. It had become heavy as if it were carrying the weight of my sorrows. I could feel every muscle in my body tense up as I wrapped my fist around the heart on the chain. What had happened? Everything I once knew had changed. A sob escaped my tightly closed lips as I pulled on the heart, yanking the necklace from my neck. I held it tightly in my hand as I processed all my emotions. I needed to let go, but how could I? I had so many questions and no answers.

Before I realized what I was doing, the sound of the metal clanking against the glass doors of the shower echoed through me as I slipped back into the dark abyss of my mind. To a memory, time, a place, where John was my father. My last thought being the only thing once meaning everything to me was hovering over the drain, just on the brink of falling into the darkness never to be seen again. Just like me.

"Bree," Dad yelled to me from the bottom of the stairs. Mom was sick again, and this time it had been a long time since she had her normal break. She would go through times when she was really sick, and then times when she was okay.

"Coming…" I called out. Pulling on a sweatshirt,. I shuffled around the corner, and down the stairs. My eyes automatically landed on my mother. Her frail body was lying on the couch, and though she was smiling, I could see this time around the treatments had been hard.

"Bree," she called out for me, her voice hoarse, as if she needed a glass of water. Dad came to stand next to me, placing a hand on my shoulder with a warm smile.

"She'll be okay, Bree," he reassured me, even though we both knew reassuring would only get us so far.

"Mom..." I said breathlessly, anxiety filled my belly sloshing around with every step I took toward her.

"Hi, sweetie. How are you? How is school?" she asked all motherly, completely ignoring the big huge elephant in the room.

"Uh...." I looked back to Dad, who gave me a reassuring smile. I wasn't sure if I should even talk to mom about anything. One thing could cause her stress and the excess stress would only make her cancer worse.

Her warm hand landed on mine as I took a seat against her body. Pushing the tears to the back of my mind, I tried my hardest to see her as I saw her when I was five. Happy, healthy, and vibrant with life.

"Tell me..." she said softly, her eyes smiling.

"Well, school is good, excellent even. My grades are good, and I was asked to the dance." I went on and on telling her the good things—the things she had missed out on because she was in the hospital.

"That is so good, I'm excited. Has dad taken you dress shopping yet?" I shook my head. The idea of going to the dance was actually the furthest thing from my mind.

"No, but I will..." Dad broke in, smiling, bringing the happiness back into the air.

"Good. Make sure she gets something sparkly... and pink... It fits her..." she mumbled her eyes glazing over. The meds must be kicking in.

"Don't worry about her, Bree. you know how she gets once the meds start working." Dad smiled, the warmth of it alone radiated to me as I gently lay her hand beside her and stood from my seat.

"Do you think she'll be okay?" I asked, looking at

*her and then back to him. The way mom had been acting
lately made it seem like she wouldn't make it. Though, I
never would say it out loud.*

*"Bree…" Dad came to stand next to me, his hand
landing on my shoulder as he turned me in toward his
chest. Without hesitation, I wrapped my arms around him.*

*"I will always be here for you. I will always care for
you, and I will always provide you with the things you need
and want. You will always be Daddy's little girl."*

*I smiled against his chest as I hugged him a little
tighter.*

*"Turn around. I have something for you," he said
softly as I turned around while he reached into his pocket.*

*Forcing myself to stay put, I waited as he placed a
small pendant against my chest. It was a gold plated heart
with little words scribbled across it.*

*"What does it say, Daddy?" I asked with excitement
and curiosity in my voice.*

*"It says 'You can always count on me.' Things are
going to get bad with Mom, but I want you always to
remember, no matter how bad they get you can always
count on me. Always." His voice cracked as he turned me
back around. This time it was he pulling me into an
embrace.*

"Always, Bree."

*I allowed his words to soothe me as I took every
single one of them in—and they did.*

I pulled myself from the memories, no longer able
to digest what had happened. If John was really so bad,
then why did he act like he cared? All those years he
pretended to be something he wasn't.

Picking up soap, I vigorously scrubbed my body,
trying to rid myself of the emotions swirling within me. I
wanted every memory of who he was scrubbed from my
mind. I wanted Zerro gone. I wanted the pain to go away. It
was completely consuming me. I should've known it was

all too good to be true.

Four days had passed since I even uttered a word to Jared or Zerro. I refused to talk to the very people who told me the things that had ripped my world apart. It was bad enough both of them played a part in the mix somehow. Zerro had killed my father, and I wasn't sure I would ever be able to handle it.

I had just walked into the bedroom we were supposed to be sharing though we weren't. I made him sleep on the couch, too afraid I might slit his throat at night while he was sleeping.

Stripping off my shirt and shorts, I stood before him in my bra and panties. I turned around narrowing my eyes, ready to head into the bathroom. Was I ready to talk about this? Ready to let it go? All I had done for the past four days was to think. Think about all the fucked up things in my life. I was being pulled in five different directions. Part of me said it was okay to love Zerro and that he had been the good guy in killing John, but there was another part of me. Part saying it was wrong, and even though he wasn't my father, I should love him regardless simply because he was there for me when no one else was.

"Bree, we should talk. Talk about everything," Zerro said. His voice was full of pain, and I'm sure if I looked at him, he would be pained by everything I was going through. It wasn't the point though. He was the cause of the pain. It didn't matter if John wasn't my dad. He had still killed someone who had raised me my entire life. He had still killed the last breathing person who loved and cared about me as much as my mother had. I had lost so much, and for what?

Turning on my heels, I looked at him. Really looked

at him. "There is nothing to talk about. The pain I see in your eyes is for yourself. For once in your life, you did something you might actually regret. You did something that broke me and ripped me from you."

I had been nothing but understanding of his need for vengeance, but somewhere inside of me, I hoped and prayed he could let it go and hoped his need for love was more than his need to shed blood. I was wrong.

Removing my bra and panties, I watched them fall to the floor, and his eyes grew wide with unknown desires. The man I had loved was standing before me… and I was bare to him as I was. Yet I still knew I would never be enough.

"We can fix this, Bree. We can be whole." His voice was pleading with me. Was he trying to save us after he had shoved us head first into this world of blood? Once something was broken, it would never be as strong as it once was. I turned the faucet on to scolding hot and jumped into the shower ignoring him.

The water burned me, it burned my skin, turning my skin red, and though it was painful, it covered everything else for a moment.

"I will not give you the fuck up, Bree. You knew my need for revenge was important. You knew if it came down to it, I would have to kill him. Look at what he did to you. Look at what he did to us— to me." Zerro practically yelled as he slipped into the shower behind me.

As much as I hated him and wanted nothing to do with him, I needed him. I needed his touch, his words, and his anger.

Turning around, I smacked him. Hard. Straight across the face. It took him by surprise and it caused my blood to pump. Some of my anger had been unveiled, and I felt the need to do it again, and again. To beat him to the bloody mess he had left my heart in.

His eyes grew wide for a moment in pure shock and

then he was on me, his lips devouring mine as he picked me up and slammed my back against the shower wall. Hot water sprayed down on us as I made him bleed in the most sensual ways. My teeth bit into his lips until I tasted blood, and my nails scraped against his back.

"Hurt me, Bree. Make me feel whatever it is you want me to feel. I'm bared to you. I know I hurt you, I know I fucked up, but it had to be done. It had to happen—and while you hate me, you'll move on and learn to deal with it. Death is the only thing promised in this life."

"I do hate you," I growled, pulling at his hair as he laid kisses against my neck. My body tingled in unimaginable ways, washing away all the anger and sadness. I would never admit it right now, but I needed him. I needed him like I needed water to drink or the air to breathe.

"Then show me. Show me how much you hate me," he whispered. His teeth grazed my ear as his cock pressed against my hot core.

With hands wrapped under my ass, he pressed into me. His cock and body promised me millions of ways to forget, and I wanted to forget. I wanted to so badly. Letting the walls fall, I reached up, gripping his face as I stared into a pair of warm eyes.

"Fuck me," I barely whispered onto his lips as if it were a secret between the two of us. Laying his head against mine, I stared into his eyes as he slid into me to the hilt. His cock felt amazing, and though my body felt as if it were crumbling, it also felt as if it was being pieced back together.

One hand slipped from my ass to my head as he gripped my hair, pulling it taut against my scalp. It burned, but it was a delicious burn. A foreign one not meant to feel good but did. My head tipped back against the tile as he pierced my skin with his teeth. His cock slipped in and out at a scary pace, and just when I was afraid I was going to die from pleasure, I came spiraling into a deep, deep darkness. My body hummed as he continued his assault on my body.

"I fucking love you, I love this sweet cunt, and I love those deep brown eyes as they smile at me when you come…" He growled into my skin. My tits rubbed against his chest, pushing me into overdrive. I wanted more, so much more.

"Stop," I begged, pulling away from him. I wanted to watch him when he took me. Shutting the water off, I slipped from his touch as I watched his face form into confusion.

"I want to watch you take me. Own me," I said quietly as I slipped from the shower and over to the counter top of the sink. A huge mirror was against the wall, and when I leaned over it and looked at him in the mirror, I watched his face light up in the excitement.

"I'll take you, I'll own you. I'll make you whole again, *Piccolo*…" His voice was on the verge of losing its gentleness, and I wanted it. I wanted the roughness. I wanted the hate and madness between the two of us to be swept away in the caresses, kisses, and bites. Sliding in behind me, I watched him in the mirror as he centered himself at my entrance.

"You better hold on, baby," was all he said as he pushed into me with sheer force. My nipples scraped across the counter top with every push into my body, and my eyes locked with his in the mirror as my teeth bit my lip to stifle my moans.

"Come on now—let that pussycat purr," he said, His tongue glided against my back as he gripped my hips harder than ever.

His dirty words pushed me over the edge and I couldn't hold in the pleasure anymore. "Ahhhh…." I mewled over and over again.

"That's what I wanted to hear," he said between

clenched teeth as a muscle in his jaw thrummed to life. I knew even he was holding back and I hated it. I wanted him. All of him.

"Fuck me, Zerro. Fuck me like you love me. Fuck me like your kiss is the last I will ever receive." Raising his eyebrow at me, a smile twitched on his lips. My blood sang, and the next thing I knew, I was flipped around sitting on the counter top, and he was fucking me, lifting me up to impale myself on his dick.

"Take it. All of it. Own me," he whispered as his dick pushed against my back wall. My muscles clamped around him and my body tingled with pulses of pleasure. My eyes drifted closed.

"Open your eyes," he growled. He wrapped his hand around my throat to force my face upward and my eyes open. Hesitantly, I open them just to watch his beautiful body on the verge of its own pleasure. His muscles were taut, and the dips and valleys of his muscles clenched together as he shoved into me once more.

A hiss escaped his lips as he gripped me hard, his seed filling me. His touch told me he was holding on for dear life, afraid I would slip away.

Pulling out of me slowly, I winced. My insides were a mushy mess, as was my heart and mind. My face was downcast as his fingers lifted my face up to his. "Run all you want, *Piccolo*. Run wherever your little legs can carry you, but realize I will always come for you. I will always find you, and I will always claim you as mine."

His words crept into my mind as I watched him reach for a towel and wrap it around himself. He left without another single word said. I wasn't sure what was meant by his words, but I knew there was no running from whatever it was we had. He would hunt me down and bring me back to him. He was right—the only thing to ever flourish from this life was death and he would be the death of me.

Inevitable

chapter six

Bree

Even after sitting in the shower until it ran cold against my skin I still didn't know what to think, what to say or how to feel. I wanted to hate Zerro, I wanted to see him drown in his own blood, but there was something more. It was as if he anchored me to the ground. Kept me sane enough to push through this mess, even if it was half his fault.

Whoever John truly was, it was a mystery. I knew John had killed Zerro's mom the moment I walked into the house. I had every intention of confronting him, but never was given the chance.

A knock on the door pulled me from my thoughts. He was probably coming to make sure I hadn't offed myself. I wasn't that dumb, I didn't want to die. I had come this far, and to throw it all away with a bullet to the head would be pointless.

"Jared wants to talk to you," Zerro said gruffly, his voice like warm honey to my body. My body responded to him even when I didn't want it to.

"Okay," I simply said pulling the bathroom door open so I could get some clothes. A shirt and pair of sweat pants sat on the bed. No panties and no bra? Hmm… Just the way Zerro liked his women, I'm sure. Not that it really mattered. I was betting they weren't expecting me.

As I slipped the towel from my body, I watched Zerro. I was done letting him be the one in control. I was done being afraid. I was tired of feeling caged, and if I couldn't get someone to give me the answers I wanted, then I would get them myself.

"What happened in there doesn't make us okay," I said sternly. I had given into my biggest weakness. Him. His eyes twinkled with amusement and a pantie-dropping smirk formed on his face as I pulled on the sweatpants.

"Right… So fucking you senseless won't make things better, but it'll get you to forget for a short time." My eyes narrowed at him. He knew I had used him as a way to let the pain go. He wasn't dumb and I didn't expect him to be. I just didn't think he had me figured out yet.

"Don't think you have me figured out because you don't," I growled, looking him straight in the eyes. He fed off breaking the weak, off making them feel as useless as he felt they were. When I looked at him, I saw a man I loved… and a man who was capable of killing me.

Taking a step forward into my space, his finger traced my bottom lip as if he were memorizing it.

"I don't think I have you figured out… I always have. There was no thinking needed. Now go," he ordered. I didn't want him to think I was listening to him, but I was eager to hear what Jared had to say and if any of it was true.

Balling my hands into fists, I pulled my shirt on ignoring him. Once fully dressed, I walked out of the room slamming the door behind me. That'll fucking teach him. As childish as it all was, I had been through so much shit. I understood his pain, the feelings he felt about losing his mom. My question was why would you want to inflict the same pain on someone you loved? Someone who had already lost so much.

"Come sit down," Jared commanded, smiling at me softly. It was impossibly hard to look at him as a half-brother or a relative at all. Passing around the leather couch, I took a chair in the corner. The cushion was soft and I sank right into it.

Training my eyes on his, I spoke softly. "I want to know everything. I want to know what happened and how we got where we are. So much shit has happened in the last month, and I don't know who to believe and who not to believe. As of right now, I have nothing to lose but my own life."

He smiled casually taking a seat on the leather couch. I wondered what our father looked like. If he looked like Jared. Hell, I wondered where he had been all these years. What he was doing when my mom was dying of cancer?

"First, as weird as this is… it's pretty cool to have a sibling. Granted, the death of John is hard on you right now. You have to know he wasn't your father, though. I know Zerro killing him made it harder than ever to deal with it, but there is more to it than what he just did to Zerro. Though he was my uncle, I still think he deserved to die."

"Uncle?" I questioned. What the hell was he talking about? John was an only child. I never met my grandparents because they were dead. When mom died, it was simply Dad… I mean John, and a few friends who came to visit.

Scratching at the back of his head as if worried, he looked at the ceiling. "Yes Uncle. As in my dad, I mean our dad and John were brothers. It explains why it was possible for him to push off you being his daughter. Now see… I know your mind is spiraling out of control, but just breathe…."

I couldn't wipe the shocked expression from my face. My jaw was practically hanging open, and an outpour of anger radiated from somewhere inside me. My whole fucking life had been a lie. A big huge fucking lie.

"My whole life was a lie…" I murmured as if in a trance. This had to be a dream, a sick and twisted dream. I was just waiting for someone to come and wake me up.

"Don't look at it like that," Jared pleaded. Lifting my gaze, I stared off into the distance. John wasn't my father, but my uncle and Jared. Alzerro's right-hand man or driver or whatever the fuck he was, was my brother.

"Did Zerro know?" I questioned. It wouldn't surprise me if he did. He knew everything. Secrets were kept deep in his mind, behind tightly closed lips.

Shaking his head, he said, "No. He didn't. There's more though. Just know none of us knew anything about this. I mean, hell, I didn't even know, Bree. Believe me when I say I'm truly sorry. I never meant for any of this to take place, and I know you have already had so much heartache this year, but know you're not alone."

"Alone," I huffed out, almost wanting to laugh a hysterical laugh—not out of laughter but craziness, because honestly, I felt like I was losing my mind.

"I mean, I know you lost John and your mother, but you have me now and our dad." The way he said all of this made it seem like I should be happy. I should have understood and to be grateful to have lost so much just to gain two people I hadn't known at all and who I knew nothing about.

"How? How did this happen? What the fuck took place for this lie to spiral years and years out of control?" I was on the verge of losing it—hell, I already had. I just wasn't sure I could come back from all of this if I did.

Smiling, Jared stood. Where the fuck was he going? "Tell me everything," I cried out as he walked into the open kitchen and grabbed a bottle of something with brown contents. My guess was whiskey, but who was I kidding—I didn't drink. Until now.

"I think we need this right now," he said walking back into the room to hand me the bottle. He had no fucking clue. Unscrewing the bottle cap, I tipped the bottle back and took a huge swig.

The sweet whiskey hit my senses and instead of a burn, I felt a deep warmth radiate through my insides settling deep into my belly. The drink had calmed me slightly, so I decided to take another swig.

"Let me start at the beginning…" Jared said watching me as I wiped away any excess whiskey. I sat the bottle on the table as Zerro emerged from the bedroom coming to a stand behind Jared.

I narrowed my eyes at him for a moment, and then allowed my anger to go as I waited for Jared to start talking.

"Your mother married John. John was, well, strange. He was a cop, and his job was to protect and serve, obviously. He took his job a little too close to the heart. He ended up in a case involving the King Family." Jared paused looking between Zerro and me. Had we been connected to one another far before our own births?

"Many of his own men, people he considered to be his best friends, were dying left and right. Killed mostly in the line of duty, but because there were many problems in the family back then, most died trying to take down The King Empire. John and your mother's marriage started out great, but then turned dark. As he became more and more consumed with finding out what he could with the King Family, he left your mom alone. Verbal abuse turned into physical abuse, and eventually, your mom was running. Running from a life she felt she had caused."

"Wait…? My mom felt she caused all these problems." I couldn't even wrap my head around this. My mother couldn't be to blame. Then again, I thought John was a perfect angel. It was all a lie.

"Just listen," Jared continued. "In the summer of 1994, your mom *fell* pregnant with you. Now, I say fell because it wasn't a planned pregnancy. Your mother had been seeing James, my father—our father, I mean," he corrected himself.

"She was seeing our father behind John's back. Most of the time, it was just out of comfort and eventually, it morphed into so much more. Anyway, John came home and found out about your mother's affair. She had to tell him she was pregnant. He would find out anyway. And thus, this started the long war of hate between the two brothers.

"Now, I'm not sure if the abuse stopped, but your mother was never allowed to tell my father. Never. John simply made her keep it secret. He threatened to take you away if she ever told. John later discovered our father was working for the King family. This only fueled his rage more. He hated Alzerro's family, so he used you. Your mother died, and he used you. He made an agreement with Alzerro putting you in the line of fire. He knew what he was doing. He just wasn't seeing it for all it was... His need for vengeance and revenge was more important than his love for a child who was never his," Jared finished, and I couldn't help but grab the bottle of whiskey again. This was too much.

Were there even words to describe how I was feeling? Zerro had killed John—someone I considered to be my father, but had he deserved it all along? Had he truthfully beat my mother, had he hurt the person I loved most and then used me for revenge?

The whiskey warmed me all over again, as my insides burned like fire. "This is so fucked up," I whispered into the air. Sitting the whiskey back down on the table, I looked over at both of them.

"How did you find this all out?" I questioned.

Jared smirked, and I knew it was going to be an interesting conversation. "Well, asshole over here couldn't handle losing you. He needed something to hold onto. I went to my father to do a little digging and he told me. Turns out, on your mother's dead bed, she let our father know. She told him everything."

I stared deeply into Zerro's eyes. In them, I could see the flames of fire flicking back and forth. He had come for me. He had wanted to save me. He may have been a man of death who held pain and heartache, but he knew love. After all, his vengeance was fueled by his love for his mother.

I took a deep breath trying to digest all of it. It felt like one of those huge pills you had to take when you were sick. The bigger the pill the harder it was to swallow.

"Let me get this straight, John and James are brothers. My mom married John, cheated on him with James because John was abusive. She then ended up pregnant with me, but only managed to stay with John because he said he would take me away. John's anger stemmed from his brother working for Zerro's family who had killed numerous colleagues of his who had tried to bring them down. My mom never told James until she was dying. John took my mom's death as a perfect chance to get revenge and made a deal with the new King of the family knowing if his life were on the line, I would step in?" My mind was reeling. I was angry, mad, sad, abused, and used. I felt not only my life had been a complete lie, but everyone I had known along the way was a lie, too.

All of this explained a lot but not soon enough. I should've known these things all along. I should've been told these things from the start. Times like now made me wish my mother was still here. Tears threatened to escape from my eyes, but I forced them back. I had been strong this far, I could go the extra mile, right?

"It's okay to be frustrated and angry about it. I know I was, our father was, Zerro was." Was he trying to justify the lies?

"It's not okay. It's not okay I was fed lies from the start and it's not okay I missed out on nearly twenty years of my life." My words twisted the knife that had been put in my chest. Saying the words made it true.

"Stop, Bree," Zerro commanded. He knew I was right there, right on the edge of a cliff ready to jump. I was feral with rage.

"No. You know nothing. You don't know what it's like. You don't know how much it hurts," I cried out as my hands gripped my hair. It was all a lie. A big huge fucking lie. It felt like everyone I had known was laughing in my face.

"Shhh," Zerro whispered in my ear as I lifted my head taking notice he had crossed the room to sit next to me. I had no words. Nothing could fix this mess, a mess that had been started far before my time.

"I can't believe…." I said in disbelief repeating the same sentence over and over again in my mind.

"You can believe it. You will believe it. You will acknowledge it and move on because you're stronger than this. You have lost so much, but you have gained so much, too." My tears secretly escaped my eyes as they slid down my cheeks like the truths that slipped from Jared's mouth.

"I'm not strong enough to do this, Zerro," I cried into his chest, allowing him to cradle me. I didn't care I was breaking down in front of Jared. I couldn't cope with this anymore. I couldn't handle the pain that shook my body.

"You're strong enough, *Piccolo*… You're stronger than anyone I know…" His voice was so gentle and made me want to beg him for forgiveness even though I knew I didn't have to. He had killed John because he deserved it.

"I hurt you… The things I said…" I cried harder

66

and tears saturated his shirt. I couldn't handle the betrayal I was feeling. John may have planned to sell me out, but Zerro had been there. I may never have been a part of his plan, but I was now… He had saved me.

"Shhhhh…. We all say things out of rage and anger. When I told you I was indebted to you, I meant it. Our fates were sealed before we were even thought of…"

"But…." I tried to say…

"No, but, Bree. Neither of us knew what was happening. I hurt you after you saved my life, and even if John wasn't your father, I know there is a part of you who loves him regardless, and I ripped that part of you to shreds. I let my anger and my need for blood to get in the way of it all. Even if he deserved to die, I shouldn't have done it that way." Regret was rooted deeply in his voice. He was never sorry. He was never caring if he ripped people from their loved ones.

"How can we move on…? So much chaos, lies, and betrayal have taken place." I was mumbling my words as I spoke into his chest. His body was warm encasing me in a protective shell. In his arms, I felt right at home as if this is where I had always belonged.

"I'm going to go call my dad," Jared said dismissing himself. I didn't look up to say anything, not even a thank you. I wasn't sure if I could ever thank him for freeing the secrets that would tear me apart only to build me back up.

"None of this is your fault, Bree. No one blames you. We had no choice in any of this. Life has a way of making choices for us." His words were making my heart pound. I gripped his shirt tighter, wondering what to do next. I had no home, nowhere to go and no family—none that I knew at least. I was supposed to be hiding, and I knew Zerro killing John put the FBI on our backs, and with Mack still looming out there somewhere, I knew our deaths would be inevitable.

"What do we do? This clusterfuck we call life is

falling to pieces before our eyes. You have lost your whole family to death, as have I. Are we next? Is this all we live for? Revenge? Hate? Anger?" I was on the verge of a panic attack. Zerro adjusted his hold on me, pushing me at arm's length so one of his hands could cup the side of my face.

"If anyone has taught me life is more than just death—it's you. Life is so much more than what I thought it was. I was simply going through the motions, breathing the air, and waiting until the last moment when my heart would stop beating. We can overcome all of this." He was convincing. He was more than convincing, but I had just been ripped apart.

"I need time. I need sleep. I need to be alone." I could barely believe myself as I said the words. I had never wanted to be alone in my life, but now more than ever I needed to be. I wanted Zerro, but I needed to piece this puzzle together. I needed to know where he and I fit in it— if we fit in it together at all.

"Okay, that's fine. Just tell me you're okay. Tell me no one hurt you while you were being hidden. Tell me everything inside of here is okay," he said pointing to my heart. Was everything okay in it? Placing his lips against my forehead, he whispered, "I know I've hurt you. I put your life in danger. I could've had us both killed numerous times. I threatened your life back at your childhood home, and I want you to know it killed me to hurt you. It ripped me apart inside. Your heartbeat is my own. Your voice my own. Your fears my own. You're mine, and I will never do anything to jeopardize that again."

His words were beautiful and heartfelt, and the tears burned down my cheeks as I pulled from his touch. I needed to get my bearings on everything, and no matter how much I wanted to believe his words right this second, I couldn't. Getting up, I turned around and walked down the hall to the room I was brought to when I first arrived. The moment I closed the door, the tears, the pain, and the earth shattering realization's hit me. This was my life now.

Inevitable

Zerro

"Fuck," I said harshly, my fist hitting the table hard. I didn't want to start breaking shit. I didn't want to hurt anyone anymore, but I couldn't handle the emotions running through me.

"Is everything okay?" Jared asked concerned as ever. He was always fucking concerned. However, now his concerns were real. I was dating his half-sister, or was I? From her words mere moments ago, I was beginning to think we had nothing. Then again, if I were just thrown the shit storm she was, I would be doing a whole lot more than just needing time.

"Everything is just fan-fucking-tastic," I scoffed, slamming back a gulp of the whiskey sitting in front of me. I needed a drink about as badly as I needed Bree's sweet lips against mine.

"I take that as she didn't take it nearly as well as I thought she would." He was joking... or trying to. It was a shame Bree had been caught up in all of this. I had taken the sweet, shy, and innocent woman I loved and morphed her into a broken killer. She was broken and it was my fault—no, it was John's fault.

"You mean you actually expected her to accept what you said right off the bat? We have bloodthirsty criminals breathing down our backs left and right, and then we have to throw shit on her. I can't even imagine what she is thinking right now," I growled out in frustration. I didn't want to be too loud, but I needed to let some of the aggression out. Killing John did nothing for me. I thought it would make me feel fuller, happier. Instead, it made me feel worse... even if he did deserve to die.

Shrugging his shoulders, he took the empty seat on the leather couch across from me. "No. I just got off the phone with my dad and he wants to meet her. I told him we found her... More like she found us, but that's beside the point. I think my dad can point us in the direction of where to find Mack."

Stretching my legs out, I settled further into the couch. Another slam back of Whiskey, another feeling escaping.

"I just feel..." I wasn't even sure where to start and why the fuck was I pouring my soul out to Jared. He didn't care.

A smirk pulled at his lips. "We both know what you feel. There isn't anything you can do to change it. I know your emotions are conflicted, but you need to give her some time. We need to let her go through everything so she's strong enough to carry on when the time comes." Was he already sticking up for her in a brotherly way? I wanted to laugh.

"Already pulling out the brother card, huh?" I said laughing.

Grinning, he shook his head. "Nah. But if you break her heart, I will probably break your face. How's that for the brotherly card?" His comment sent a spiral of happiness to form within. Bree may have lost so much, but she had gained so much, as well. Jared, a person who would be a better brother to her than anyone I knew. James, a father who would claim her as his own. And me—a man, who against all odds, had opened his heart to love.

"I would love to see you try and break my face," I taunted knowing very well even Jared wouldn't be able to take me down. He could say he would all he wanted, but I knew better.

Rolling his eyes like a girl, he laughed. "Whatever. That's not the point, asshole. The point is you know we lost my mom. It has only ever been my dad and me, and I don't want to go into pussy foot country and spill my guts to you, but to have someone else is just... exhilarating. For the first time in years, my dad is moving around again. He's coming here to see her, and though the truth was a damn—nation to her, it was a joy to us."

The faraway look in his eyes told me he was going back there. I knew the look. I had endured it many times. He had lost his mother, too. Not to the same fate I had, but far worse. There was nothing to stop what had happened to his mother.

"It's okay, Jared." I tried to sound convincing, but he knew when to call my bluff, and there would be no better time to do so than now. I was a hypocrite. I knew it. I told people to move on from their own problems while I still boiled in my own.

"Just make sure she's okay enough to talk later," he said blinking slowly as if he were trying to bring himself back to the present. He couldn't still blame himself for her death. It wasn't his fault. He was just a kid.

"It wasn't your fault, Jared," I said surprising even myself. I never stepped into the arena with him. I never tried to be the friend he needed. Turning on his heels, I saw a deep anger rooted in his eyes.

Clenching his teeth, he spoke forcefully. "Take your own advice, Zerro. Don't try to tell me how to handle my shit when you're barely getting by with your own struggle."

What was I supposed to say to that? Nothing, that's

what, so I did just that. I let him walk away, down the hall to his room, leaving me to sit in the emptiness to think about all the fucked up choices I had made. Funny, when you're alone, your mind tends to wander. I started to wonder if everything would come out okay, if we all would get our happily ever after, or if we all were headed down the road to war. Only time would tell.

Hours had passed as I continued to sit in the chair across from her watching her sleep. Her body was worn and tired, her breaths were deep, and her chest rose and fell in rhythm with my own beating heart. This moment took me back to the very last time we had sex—when we were on good terms. How I had awoken her from a very similar position.

"*Ride my hand, baby…*" My own words echoed through my mind as I remembered every push and pull of our bodies. The way we became one, how I would've loved to do nothing but stay wrapped up in who she was for hours. Then I think I would've given everything up for her. Hell, I still would, but things were different now. Death changed people. It changed things. Technically, we're still enemies, but for her to be one, Jared would have to be one, too. I could never turn my back on them.

A deep moan pulled me from my thoughts as I watched Bree roll over in bed. She was wearing one of my shirts and a pair of my boxers. Her shirt was riding up on her back, and her lower back and ass were showing.

My cock was stiff and ready to take her. Of course, it was always hard with her around, but there was something so much more important that needed to be handled. I needed to know what had happened to her while she was gone. Where she had been taken, all she had endured. God, I was a fucking douche bag for not asking these questions before doing anything with her.

Ringing my hands together, I clasped them in front of me. Did I really want to talk to her about all of this? I know I had said how sorry I was, but I needed to know she was okay. I needed to make this right.

Slipping from the chair, I tiptoed across the floor and to the bed. For a moment in time, I stood staring at her beautiful face. It was more than the face of an angel. It was the face of my savior. The woman I loved, who I had hurt, betrayed, and somehow, still managed to keep. Her nose scrunched together as if she was having a bad dream and her pink lips parted a sigh escaping.

Right then, my heart did a little pitter patter. Yes, the totally fucking girly kind where sighs fall from lips and eyelashes bat. I was pussy whipped and I didn't even care. Not one fucking bit.

"Hey, *Piccolo…*" I whispered against her skin as I clasped the side of her cheek gently. She stirred only slightly and one eye opened.

"It's still dark out, so if you're waking me up, somebody better be dying. Wait—no, scratch that… somebody had better not be dead. Too much heartache going on around here." I could tell by the humor lacking in her voice she wasn't kidding.

"I just needed to talk to you. I needed to let you know your father, Jared's dad, is coming to meet you. I know you said you needed some time to digest everything that had happened, but we don't really have time. We need to devise a plan and…" I trailed off. I was the motherfucking king, but here I was bowing to her. Putting myself on the line. I had never had to ask someone if things were okay between us—simply because I never cared enough to ask.

"And?" she asked puzzled as I sat on the bed next to her. My dick was still hard, and the way she was looking at me was making it more difficult for me to focus on the task at hand. Fuck. *Yeah, that's what you needed to be doing...*

"And.... I need to know...." Pause. "If everything between us...." Pause again. Would I ever be able to fucking man up? Fuck having a cock—if I looked down, I guarantee I would have found a pussy since I was acting like one.

Sighing, I looked her straight in the eyes as if I were looking straight down the barrel of a gun. "I need to know we're okay. I know it sounds fucked up, but I need to know you're all right. I need to know you aren't lost somewhere in that pretty fucking head of yours." She knew what I was asking because not even a second passed before she started giving me answers.

"Well, basically, I was held in a hole for three weeks. When I say hole, I do mean one in the ground, surrounded by dirt. I was talked down upon and treated like shit for hours upon hours. Then... someone who says he knows you baited me to get out of the hole. Technically, I baited him, but it doesn't matter..." Closing my eyes for a moment, I took a deep breath to calm myself. If he touched her, there was a cement block with his name on it.

"Anyway, I got out of the hole with the intent of running or doing whatever I could to escape. Instead of having to fight him though, he just kind of let me go..." She sounded surprised, which in turn kind of surprised me. Why the hell would they let her go? There had to be a motive.

"Who was this man? What did he look like? Did he touch you?" The questions came out rushed, and I felt myself reaching out to touch her, simply in relief to remind myself she was here. I was a pussy. A total fucking pussy. Next thing you know, I would be watching The Notebook and talking about The Vampire Diaries.

Smiling, a sexy as all fucking hell grin, she said, "Relax, Mr. King. Nothing happened. He didn't hurt me. He was wearing a mask and didn't give me his name, but he did have super green eyes. Like the greenest eyes I have ever seen, and he told me something…" Seconds passed as I watched her work through her thoughts.

"He told me something about thanking you, and he was returning the favor. Something like that. It was odd, but I wasn't going to stick around and ask questions. He told me to run and that's what I did." Inwardly, I sighed in relief. My mind suddenly wandered to a green-eyed boy I had as Intel. Devon? Was that his name? It had been forever since I last talked to him. I had cleaned him up, gave him a place to stay, and took care of him for months. In return, he would feed me information pertaining to the cops, FBI—you name it. Maybe I needed to pay Devon a little visit.

"Where did this all come from?" she asked pulling the sheet up as she sat up. Her dark brown eyes were anything but doe-like anymore. Everything that seemed shy and unknown had been explored. She was strong, so fucking strong, and she was mine. All mine.

"Bree. I love you. I loved you the moment I met you. I simply didn't understand what it was that drew me to you. I fought my own men and broke all my own rules to be with you. I may have killed and been ruthless. I may have been the monster everyone makes me out to be, but I never stopped loving you."

Her eyes welled up with huge tears. I wanted to reach out and comfort her, but for what? For being honest and for telling her how much she means to me? Fuck no. One single tear slipped from her eye and fell to her cheek where it slid down ever so slowly.

"I don't want you to think I don't want you or care about you because I do. I know why you killed John. I understand it was needed on your part, but it's going to be hard for me to forget it. It doesn't matter how evil someone is. If you loved them even the tiniest bit, you'd always remember the love, above all else." I understood what she meant. It was similar to how she felt about me. She could always remember the good things I had done over the bad. Even when the bad outweighed the good by a million. She had a heart of gold while I had a cold, dark one.

"It just seemed like…" I said ashamedly. I had never worked through such emotions.

"Look at me, Zerro…." she said cupping my cheek to turn my face into hers. I didn't resist her touch. "I want to be with you, I want to find out answers, too. We're a team. We can do this together."

"Is this your way of saying you thought everything through? I'm really sorry…" I pleaded. I hated feeling lower than dirt. I had never felt this way before.

"I'm okay. I'm not great or fabulous, but I'm capable of moving from what happened."

I smiled, unable to hide the happiness. "I bet you I can make you feel great, maybe even fabulous?" I teased wiggling my eyebrows at her. One time, two times... hell, a million fucking times would never be enough for me. She had me wrapped around her finger and every inch of me called to her. She simply smiled, which caused my heart rate to accelerate…

"Shouldn't you be devising some insane, off the wall, guns a blazing attack plan?" Her teeth sank into her full, pale pink lips, and I was more than ready to lose all my clothes and attack her like an animal.

Tugging at my shirt, I smiled. "Gun's a blazing sounds fun, but fucking you until you can't walk or talk sounds better, doesn't it?" I growled. With my shirt off, I started to tug on my pants but was stopped by two small hands.

"Let me," she said pulling at the button on my jeans. Her smile was a killer, making my already hard cock harder—if that were even fucking possible. Loosening the button, I watched her pull the sides of my pants down.

"Commando, huh?" She laughed as her brown eyes

twinkled in the light. She was beautiful and far too fucking smart of a woman then to be caught up with me. Shimmying out of my pants, I bent down to lay claim on her. I wanted her lips, her panting breaths, and her skin against mine until the sun came up.

"What can I say? I'm always ready for you," I teased. My teeth nipped at her bottom lip. Her eyes turned to molten lava in an instant. I had the same effect on her she had on me.

"I missed you so bad…" I practically panted as my hands drifted under her shirt. I was a thirsty man. It felt as if I hadn't had a drink from her beauty in months. I was starved.

Her lips found mine, devouring the very small amount of space separating us. Her urgency turned into mine, and in a matter of seconds, I had pulled her shirt off and moved us to a sitting position. She was straddling me and I was ready for her.

"Are you ready for me, Mr. King?" she asked as one of her fingers reached out tracing over my bottom lip. The temptation to reach out and bite her was strong, but I wanted to go easy on her. I wanted to give her the control.

Looking down, my eyes glided over her body. Her full tits were on display for me, and I couldn't stop myself from palming them.

"I've missed this, you… all of it…" She seemed to purr as she arched into my touch.

"I bet you have, baby," I said, moving one hand from her tit to between her legs. One stroke of my finger told me she was soaked for me. My Piccolo was a very dirty girl.

"You're ready for me already?" I asked, laying hot kisses against her chest and neck. She pushed her dark locks to the side to give me more access, and it was then I saw the bruises on her shoulder. They were small and insignificant to the naked eye, but to the King, they were anything but.

"Who did this to you?" I asked anger filling my voice. Her expression turned from lust to confusion in mere seconds as she looked down to see what I was talking about. Fear rooted itself deep in my belly. Was she only telling me a half truth?

"I... I don't know where those came from, Zerro..." Her eyes pleaded with me to understand, and looking up at her, I knew she was telling me the truth. She wasn't sure how she had been bruised. Had I done that to her? It could very well be possible?

"Shhhh... I'm sorry I scared you..." I whispered, laying soft kisses against the bruises. I wanted them to go away. I never wanted a single thing to blemish her beautiful skin.

From there, I trailed my kisses over her neck, and down her chest, listening to her breathe and to her heart accelerating.

"Being with you is like being on a roller coaster. The moments of fear when you don't know what's around the next corner. The feeling of falling, just for a fraction of a second, where you think death may finally get you. You make me feel all of it...." she said softly, her voice as smooth as silk.

Her words stirred something deep within, and I lost control. She always brought unknown emotions to the surface. My fingers delved into her skin as I traced her entrance. So wet, so fucking wet for me.

"Fuck my finger..." I demanded gritting my teeth, as I watched her eyes light up like a fireworks show. With one hand wrapped around her chin to keep her eyes on mine, I slammed my finger into her over and over again until she found her own rhythm.

"I need more..." Panting, she pleaded with me to give her what she wanted.

"Beg for it... Show me what that sweet pussy of

yours wants," I said nipping at her lip. A frustrated sigh erupted from within her, and her movements became jerky.

"Beg for it, and I'll give you what you crave. You know my cock only wants you…" I murmured on the verge of coming myself. She was a goddess, and her body worked in so many fucking mysterious ways. I know I said I wanted her to do the pace and to be in control, but that was before she said what she said.

"Please, Zerro…" she cried out… begging, pleading, and giving me exactly what I wanted.

"Please what? You want me to fuck that dirty cunt of yours? You want my cum to fill you to the brim? Do you?" I smirked adjusting myself for her entrance the moment the words escaped her lips.

"Please, fuck me… Fuck me NOW!" She all but screamed impatiently.

"Now, now. Don't make demands, my greedy girl…" I growled at her and withdrew my finger before sliding deep into her pussy. One swift movement was all it took to get her mouth to shut. My body shuddered with the need to slam into her repeatedly, but I stood my ground, relishing every jerk and clench of her body.

Our bodies were connected, and as she slid over my cock slowly, I took the time to explore her body, leaving a path of fiery kisses over every inch of her body.

"Ahhh… Ahh…" she exclaimed, her hips moving in motion with mine as I lay back slowly to watch her work her magic.

"Fuck, yeah…" I hissed out, my hands moving to her hips. Our flesh was smacking against one another as she fucked me into oblivion. Her walls clamped onto my cock like a vise as I continued to push into her deeper than I ever had before.

"Never enough… Never enough…" I said breathlessly as my cum hit the back of her pussy and my toes curled. They literally fucking curled.

Bree's body lay against mine as we both came down from our highs listening to one another's hearts beat.

One of my hands moved of its own accord as if it had been doing this for years. I pushed the hair off her shoulder and rubbed small circles into her back. She was mine. She was all fucking mine, and I was the luckiest man in the world. It didn't matter I had lost everything to my name or I could be killed at this very moment—because I had found my home in her arms.

"Promise me, through all of this, even if Mack wins, you'll run. You'll push on for something more because both you and I know someone's going to die. Death is inevitable in the world we live in, and even if I die, I just want to know you will find your peace."

If all else failed, peace was what I wanted her to have. I wanted her to be able to move on without me.

"If I promise this to you, then you have to promise the same to me. It's not just your life on the line but both of ours." She was right, but she didn't realize I would do everything in my power to make sure she made it out, even if it meant giving up my own life for hers.

"I promise…" I lied. I couldn't promise something like that. Hopefully, it never came down to the moment where time stood still between us. If I had to, I would take the bullet for her.

"Good," she mumbled into my chest, and as much as I wanted to whisper those three little words, I knew she knew without me even having to say a thing.

chapter eight

Bree

I was wrapped in a casing of warmth. My body shuddered against another, and for one single moment, I forgot where I was. Memories swirled in my mind resurfacing in an instant. None of it was a dream. It was all a big huge reality. I didn't lie when I said I was okay—I was. But would I ever be back to the person I was before all of this? No. There was no going back to the lie that was my life.

My eyes adjusted to the darkness, and as I peered out the window, I took in the fact it was still dark. What time was it?

"The sun hasn't risen yet," Zerro said softly, his voice full of sleep. He placed a kiss on my shoulder, and I swear to God, I melted. We had made love last night, not the kinky kind, not the fuck me against the wall kind, but the slow and sensual kind. The kind that made you not two separate people, but one whole.

"What time is it?" I asked rolling over from my

stomach to face him. Today would be one of the hardest days ever. I had come to terms with what Zerro had done to John. I realized he was the bad man in all of this, but somehow, I felt as if I were sleeping with the enemy.

"My phone says four-thirty a.m." He yawned, apparently still very much tired. I rolled my eyes, even the king of Mafia had a weakness—sleep.

Laughing, I slipped the sheet from my body and pulled myself out of his warm embrace. There was no way I could sleep another minute.

"What's going on inside of that head of yours?" he asked. He had been asking a lot lately as if he thought I was unstable or something...

"Just absorbing things and wondering where I go from here." It was an honest answer. I knew I would have to talk to Jared's dad, *my dad*... soon. I would have to fill in the missing pieces somehow.

"James will have some answers for you I hope. I'm not sure where he got all his information, but I guess your mom had told him before she passed away." The air in my chest sat suspended for a second. Talking about my mom's passing hurt more than anything. Even more so now since I had no way of getting answers to the questions I desperately needed.

"I miss her..." I said aloud. I didn't mean to, but apparently, my conscious slipped.

"I know you do, and I miss mine, too." He sounded in pain, so I turned around to see his face. In his eyes, I could see the terror that was always hidden. In the place of the man I loved was the fragile, small boy hiding in a closet. I had been told the story by Mack while he kept me hostage.

"Zerro..." I tried to stop him from heading down memory lane, but it didn't work. We were two very different people living similar lives. Our pasts matched perfectly—we both had more questions than we had answers.

"People thought I just liked to kill others like it was part of the act. They didn't know why though. They didn't know it was my own personal hell or how every drop of blood that touched my skin soothed the monster inside of me. I killed because I had to. It was the only thing I knew." His voice was rising, and I could tell he wasn't with me in the room anymore. At least, not in his mind.

"I'm sorry we both have to deal with this," I said remorsefully. I was more than sorry.

"Never be sorry, *Piccolo…* the people who have made us suffer the most will soon be the ones suffering." A seductive smirk pulled at his lips. It had reminded me of a lion right before it sank its teeth into its prey.

"Good," I simply said. I slipped into a pair of sweats and one of Zerro's shirts I had found on the ground. I needed coffee and something greasy, like, now.

The house was quiet as I tiptoed out into the living room and headed for the kitchen. I looked at the coffee pot sitting on the counter and smelled the air as the sweet aroma of coffee hit my nose. Turning around, I saw Jared leaning against the wall casually as he smirked at me.

"Good morning, I presume?" Jared asked. I ignored him for the time being as I grabbed a coffee cup from the cabinet above my head. I poured myself coffee, and then headed toward the table where I noticed a cup of cream and sugar.

"You know ignoring me right now doesn't make it better. It sure as hell doesn't change things." I mixed all the ingredients in the cup and waited until I took the first sip to respond to him. I pulled the cup to my lips and sucked in a small taste, savoring the sweetness of the cream and sugar on my lips.

"I'm not ignoring you, Jared. I'm just dealing with everything. I'm absorbing it all, simply because there isn't any fucking thing else that can be done."

"Our father is coming today. He says he has something for you and it might bring you more closure." Taking another sip of the coffee goodness before responding again, I wanted to laugh. More closure? As If I had been given closure to begin with.

"Technically he is YOUR father, Jared. Not mine. As far as family is concerned, I have no one. I know you're my half-brother and by blood, he is my father. Those things don't change what has happened, though."

He snorted. His eyes looked wild. "You think I don't know that, Bree. How do you think all of this makes us feel? I mean, seriously? We're in the middle of a full out war and we find this out."

"I know what we're up against, Jared. You forget I have been—" In a moment's time, he crossed the room and came to stand right in front of me.

"I didn't forget what you looked like when I picked you and Zerro up on the side of the road. I didn't forget I had lost so much, and I didn't forget my mom had died. None of those things have changed—even though God continues to throw more shit my way."

When the words 'death' and 'mom' fell from his lips, I looked up into a face I thought I knew. It was very apparent to me, though we all seemed to be doing okay on the outside, we were truthfully each fighting our own demons. There might have been a war raging between families, but there were bigger wars waging within each of us.

"I'm so—"

"Don't even say it. We both know we've heard the words *I'm sorry* a million times. It doesn't help heal the pain. I'm just telling you this because our father hasn't had anything truthfully to live for in years. He didn't even know where you were. He knew about you but had no idea where you were." Jared sounded tortured, and my heart started to ache.

"I didn't… I had…"

"We know you didn't know. We never expected you to have a clue. I know you have been through so much, Bree. I know everything has been thrown at you at once, but I'm begging you to see things for more than they are."

"I'll talk to him, Jared. I never said I wouldn't. It just breaks my heart how my mom isn't here to answer my questions. It hurts me to know my life was a lie and there's not a damn thing to fall back on."

"Well, buck up, Princess, because it's about to get ten times harder," Jared said. There was no emotion in his voice, but I knew my words had made him feel better.

"Thanks, asshole," I said before taking another sip from my cup. I was getting anxious. I wanted answers, but I was also afraid. I wanted to run. To hide.

"Anytime. How are things with you and Zerro?" Jared asked nonchalantly as if he didn't know we were hooking up.

"We're fine. I understand his need for revenge. There wasn't anything I could do anyway. I need to be strong, and I'll hold onto my strength until I can't anymore."

He smiled, rubbing a hand over his face. He still had stubble, and the bags under his eyes said he was stressing over something at night instead of sleeping.

"Yeah, you sounded *fine*, last night…" he teased. My cheeks reddened. I wasn't a prude, but with Jared considered family, it was quite strange to know he heard us having sex.

"Ahh, don't be shy about it. Not like Zerro ever was," he joked. I turned my face away from him and out toward the rising sun. I wasn't even sure where we were anymore. All I knew was we were forty miles from my father's house. North, East, South, or West, I wasn't sure.

"Ha. Good to know, I guess." I tried to joke as well, easing all the tension from the room.

"I'm going to make breakfast. You hungry?" he asked.

"Fuck, yeah, I am," Zerro chimed in his voice causing a cascade of goose bumps to form over my body.

Jared shook his head, causing dark locks to fall to his forehead. "I bet you are. I heard you last night…"

"Oh, really. I bet it wasn't me you heard, but your little sis over there…" Zerro commented, throwing a wink in my direction. I couldn't help the smile that popped onto my face. It felt strange being able to be happy after what I had been through.

"Ha. Don't even bring *that* up." Jared got up from the table and headed for the fridge. I just stood there ogling at Zerro, who was shirtless. His hair was in a fuck-me kind of way sideways, and his body didn't look a bit damaged, even though he had taken numerous bullets. I was stunned he had lived at first, but something in me told me he couldn't have died. I would've known.

Jared's phone rang, and my attention automatically slipped from Zerro to him. He answered it within a second bringing the phone to his ear.

"Dad," he said coolly. I pretended as if I wasn't listening to the conversation, but Zerro caught me out of the corner of his eye.

"Eavesdropper…" he teased, grabbing an apple from the fruit dish in the center of the table. His mouth opened showing white teeth as he took a chomp out of the apple.

"Yeah, 102 Hickory Lane, right past the Piggly Wiggly, and left at the gas station," Jared rambled. He must be giving him directions. Weird how I hadn't noticed any of those things as we passed them.

"Don't be nervous, *Piccolo*," Zerro said calmly as if he was trying to calm my raging nerves.

"I'm not…" I lied, forcing my attention to something else. I was tired of talking about me.

88

"He is a nice man, I promise you," Zerro said, taking another enormous bite of the apple. Only he could make eating an apple look sexy.

"You know him?" I asked. I wasn't aware Zerro had met him. Hell, I wasn't aware of a lot of things.

"Yes. Jared's family and mine go way back. No worries, love, you'll be fine." He sent me one of those smiles that made my knees weak before he got up from the table and tossing the apple in the garbage all at once.

"I have to shower. I'll be back." And just like that, he was gone.

"Yup, see you soon," Jared said hanging up the phone. See you soon? Gah. This meant I would come face to face with my real father soon.

The rest of the afternoon passed with ease. I set in the living room most of the time reading. I was bored, and basically, on house arrest. At least, until we got rid of Mack and the FBI.

I was told not to turn the news on, but I did anyway. It turned out I shouldn't have. John, my so-called father's face was plastered on the screen. The news channel was talking about his murder, and how the FBI was on the lookout for anyone with any answers to how his death came about. I had two words for them—Alzerro King. Though I'm sure they knew it already.

"He's here," Jared said from across the room as he paced the floor for the twentieth time. My stomach was in knots by the time I heard the doorbell ring, and I was about ready to vomit on the floor the second I heard his greeting. It sounded unlike anything I had ever heard.

"Son," my dad said as he greeted Jared. His voice was a mixture of honey and gravel mixed together.

"Dad," Jared said in a joking manner, wrapping his

father in a tight hug. I stayed seated not sure if I should really get up or not. Not sure if my legs would really carry me or not.

They walked through the entryway, and his dark eyes slid across the room until they landed on me. He looked very similar to John in many ways, which made sense because they were brothers. His eyes were dark, his face worn, and his eyes held a look of sadness in them. They brightened slightly upon landing on me, but otherwise, he looked like a man who was born on hard times.

His body was lean and large. He had to be close to six-foot-two, if not taller.

"Bree?" he said. My name was completely unnatural to his tongue. His words shook as if he was in a state of shock. Smiling softly, I stood, taking small steps to where he was standing. As I grew closer to him, I took notice of the color of his eyes, and how they matched my own. His nose was the same shape as mine, and like a small child, I had to stop myself from tracing the similarities on his face.

"That's me," I said almost shy like. I wasn't ever shy, scared shitless maybe, but shy? No. That girl was long gone.

In a moment's time, I was wrapped in his arms as he reached out, pulling me into his arms. His body encompassed my small frame as the smell of smoke and cologne hit me.

"I can't believe it, I'm so sorry." He sounded on the verge of tears, which was strange because he didn't seem as if he were a man who often cried.

"Let's go sit and talk," Jared suggested ushering us into the living room. James released me with hesitation as if he thought I would skip away into the fog. He stared at me for a long moment, simply smiling. His eyes looked glassy, and as soon as he blinked, it disappeared. I turned around on my heels and headed for the same seat I had before.

"I can't even believe this… I'm so flabbergasted," James said shocked as if he couldn't really believe I was here.

"Don't worry, you weren't the only one shocked as all hell," I added, looking over at him as he took the seat next to me. The leather against my skin was the only thing keeping me in place. I was honestly scared to find out about the past.

Smiling, he cocked his head. "You look just like your mother—God, Samantha was beautiful." I could hear the reminiscence in his voice.

"Thanks," I said, unsure of what else there was to say. I was slightly angry he wasn't there for her upon her death and hadn't come for me.

"I'm so sorry about missing all these years. Your mother never told me about you. She just kind of disappeared, and then suddenly, she was sick, and…" He stopped midsentence seeing the sadness seep onto my face.

"It's still kind of hard to talk about her."

"Of course, of course," he said running a hand through his dark brown hair. He shared the same hair color as Jared and me, which made me think back to what Jared had said about losing his own mother. Our father had lost two loves in his life. His heartache ran deep.

"Well, Dad, I'm glad you made it here in one piece. I wasn't sure your beat up truck was going to make it through a two-hour trip," Jared joked to break the silence. We all let out a laugh as I listened to the two of them make digs at each other about the mysterious truck Jared said made it through The Cold War, World War One and Two, and Vietnam. Basically, it was old.

"Zerro," James greeted Zerro, seeing him before I did as he walked into the living room. He was wearing a pair of blue jeans and a white V-neck T. He looked fuckable. It had to be my emotions or something because I was contemplating taking him in the back room to blow off some of my nerves.

"James," Zerro greeted back in typical male fashion. Men were weird. How was stating their first name to someone considered a greeting?

"I hope you're treating my daughter well." Darkness descended on us, and my insides screamed for me to say something. After all, it was the first time he had ever laid claim to me.

"As good as a Queen should be treated." I didn't have to look at Zerro to know there was a dark look on his face. He didn't like people assuming he treated me like dirt. He didn't like anyone thinking shit about him.

"Good. I came here to talk to Bree and it's what I would like to do right now if it's okay with all of you," James said commanding all the attention. It was strange how the energy in the room changed. It didn't feel as if it was filled with testosterone, but more so with respect.

Jared and Zerro nodded their heads at the same time. "Yeah, I was just going to get Jared to watch a movie," Zerro said, his eyes zeroing in on Jared. There was a look exchanged between the two that had me wondering—were they actually watching a movie or doing recon to figure out what Mack was up to?

Even though I wanted to say something, I didn't. Instead, I let them walk away leaving me with a man who I was supposed to call my father.

"Here," James said, reaching into the front pocket of his jacket. He pulled out a white piece of paper folded many times. He extended his hand to give it to me, but I paused for a moment. What was he giving me?

"What is it?"

"A letter from your mother. She gave it to me on the rare occasion I ever saw you after her death. She told you were okay and I wasn't to go out looking for you. She said if you wanted to know about me, you would come to me."

He may have been able to hide it from others, but the hurt in his voice told me my mother's words had hurt him to the core.

"Have you read it?" I asked, taking the note from him. I didn't know if I wanted to open it here and read it.

"No, I haven't. It's addressed to you, and I wasn't going to overstep my boundaries." At least he was honest. The paper was a nice kind, the kind you would write official letters on and shit.

I unfolded it like a present on Christmas morning. I wanted—no, needed to read this note. If anything, I knew it held some type of answer.

Dearest Bree,

It saddens me deeply you won't see this letter until well after I am gone. As I lay here beside you watching you sleep, I write this with tears streaming down my cheeks. My heart is breaking for the pain I know I will cause when you finally discover my biggest kept secret. I truly hope this letter finds you in good times. Please know I never meant to hurt you in any way. I kept this secret in order to protect you.

I grew up loving two people, but the love I had for each was quite different. Falling for John was easy. He was alluring and charming, but it wasn't the kind of love I felt for James... his brother. James made me fall without even realizing it. So, if I wanted to stop it, I never had the chance. He was simply mesmerizing. Looking back now, I know I should have chosen James from the very beginning, but the love I had for John felt as if it was good enough.

John was my safe place when I needed to hide, so I stayed with him and we started our life together. Those were our best years. Those were the years when I still knew him. He always had dreams to become a police officer, and when he finally graduated from the academy, he became a different person. Little by little, it was like something changed inside of him. He became more and more wrapped around his cases. His choices changed, and his beliefs became more about his career. He stopped giving me the love and respect I deserved. I was put on the back burner, and my complaints went unnoticed. If they were noticed, it was with a fist. The bruises eventually faded, slowly taking the love I had for him with them.

This ultimately pushed me into James's arms. He was always there, witnessing the changes in his brother, as well. I felt as if I had lost my husband. In all honesty, at this point, he was already dead to me. When James lost his wife, I was there for him, and through this, we reconnected. What started as two friends being there for each other turned into something more. We became one. The magnetic pull we always had for each other came back even stronger. We knew it wasn't right, but the heart wants what the heart wants, and our hearts wanted each other.

I found myself falling completely out of love for John, and when he discovered the affair, my life shattered. He knew James had a connection to a particular case he was assigned, so he threatened him and accused him of rash things. He told me I couldn't leave him, and if I tried, he would kill me. He had so much rage in his eyes when he spoke those words to me; I knew he meant every single one of them. I became a shell of myself not living, only existing.

Then I found out about you, Bree, and you changed everything in my life. You gave me a reason to do more than simply exist. John loved you, you were his Princess, but... he wasn't your father. He knew this from the moment I told him about you, yet he always treated you as his own. I never understood why, but I guess, in a way, you were part of him just the same. My only regret is I never had the chance to let James know before John took me away.

I hope you can see the resemblance between the two of you. I always did. Countless times, I would get lost in your eyes because they reminded me of him, of the love we shared. I loved him, I always will, and somehow, I know I always did. I am still just as much in love with him now as I was then.

When I was diagnosed with cancer, I looked for him. I needed to tell him. This wasn't something I could die knowing. I know you're hurting beyond repair, but please know it was never my intention. You're strong, and I know eventually, you will see this through. Know you were made out of love and it wasn't his fault I hid you from him. Whatever you do, don't hate him. He doesn't deserve it.

I am sorry for keeping this from you, for being the person who hurt you the most. One day, I hope you will be able to forgive me. I love you in mind, body and spirit. Nothing could ever separate me from you. I'll always be in your heart.

P.S. I hope you live, never simply exist...but LIVE.

With love,
Mom

My tears stained the white paper smearing the words slightly as I folded it up. She never meant to hurt us, but she did. Now she wasn't here to fix the problems she had caused. I was a casualty of a war started years before my time. I would be the one to end this war.

"I'm so sorry, Bree." James, my father's voice, sounded from somewhere. It could've been right in front of me—hell if I know. My heart was breaking. I felt like I was a million miles away.

It was as if I knew the fate, I knew what the letter would contain, but I didn't want to believe. Even after reading it, I didn't want to believe it. I couldn't because believing it made it real and making it real made everything before this time a lie.

"Jared. Zerro." I heard James yell but felt nothing. My body was numb, and my mind lacked words. There were no words for this.

I watched as Zerro rushed in, his hands and mouth moving a hundred miles an hour. None of it mattered, though. Deep inside of me, something was happening, something similar to an earthquake. I was cracking— breaking.

His arms wrapped around me, and I was moving. He carried me to the bedroom, laying me down on the bed. He continued to shout demands at whoever would listen as I blacked out every word he said.

"Talk to me, Bree. Say something, anything," he pleaded, shutting the door to our room. What could I say? What would I say? I was numb? I was lost in the sea of lies.

Tears streamed down my face, making their own river.

"Are you in shock? What the fuck is going on, Bree? You're scaring me." I wanted to say *good*. Who could I blame? My mother was dead. John was dead. Mack was the only living evil next to Zerro, and though I was losing it, I knew my heart belonged to him. I stayed silent, replaying the letter over in my mind.

"Bree, fucking talk to me," Zerro shouted. His hands dug into my shoulders as he shook me trying to get any response he could. Did he know? I had no way of knowing if he did or not. I had no way to know what was true and wasn't.

"Lies upon lies. AND then more fucking lies. My whole life was one gigantic fucking lie. Selfishness got in the way of it all." I cried, my anger shattering the air in the room. Zerro's eyes grew large as he watched me sit up. He covered the remaining steps separating us before coming to stand in front of me.

"It's a lie!" I screamed, shoving him with my hands. He stood there like a brick wall, which just added more fuel to my fire.

"She should've told me. She should've fucking said something. She shouldn't have died and left me here without answers. She thought a fucking piece of paper would do justice…" I pounded my fists against his chest at his unemotional state, the anger inside of me swelling.

"Why are you just standing there, say something, or get out!" I growled glaring at him. I was broken. I was so fucking broken. The pieces of me shattered along with everything else that made me who I was.

"You're hurting. You want something to take it out on. If you want to hurt me, then do it." Those are the only words he said as he started at me, black opals shining in the light. The brown of his eyes were lost in the black.

"Hurt you? Who do you think I am?" I stood, pushing him back and away from me. I couldn't handle the closeness right then. I couldn't handle anything. I lied and said I had a grasp on things, but we both knew I didn't.

"You're Bree fucking Forbes. You're having a meltdown, now pummel me to the ground. Work out this fucking anger and sadness," he growled. He was feeding off me. I gritted my teeth, looking him straight in the eyes.

"You're feeding off me, using me. You're as bad as they are," I said, taking the steps needed to get in his face. I felt his hot breath against my cheek, but I didn't care. If I were broken, I didn't want to be alone in the act.

"Stop twisting this into something it isn't," he seethed, anger just on the surface of overflowing.

"Oh, but it is. Twisting it would have to make it untrue. You knew, didn't you? You knew all along?" I growled, smacking his face with the side of my hand. Bubbles of anger simmered within me.

His jaw clenched as he ground his teeth together. One of his hands snaked out, gripping my hair. It pulled tightly against my scalp, and I hissed, releasing a bit of pain. Leaning into my face, he tilted me up to look at him.

"Never accuse me of doing or knowing something you damn well know I could never keep from you." His tone was off the rails, animalistic by nature.

Leaning even closer to him, almost causing our lips to touch, I said, "I didn't accuse you of shit. I stated a fact!" The words spat from my mouth, and the second they left it, I was flying. For one moment, I was freighted. My body was airborne, and as I landed on the bed with precision, my breaths came in as pants and my chest heaved with anger.

"How dare you!" I growled, trying to get up but was only able to make it a foot before Zerro's body leaned over mine, trapping me.

"Were going to play a game, Bree. We're going to get rid of all of this anger, and the best way I see fit is to fuck. So tell me—top or bottom?"

Zerro

Her body quivered with a need for release. It wasn't just the sex though; this was the mental kind of release. Her breakdown was coming, and it wasn't going to be anything like when you came during sex.

"Get the fuck away from me." She hissed like a cat. She reminded me of a trapped animal. Her eyes were empty and her anger was coming forth. You know what it's like when you're caught between wanting to give up and wanting to cry, but still hold onto hope? That's where she was.

"The only place I'm going is inside of you." I smiled like a prick, my arms trapping her so she was unable to move. Whatever was going on inside of that pretty head of hers had nothing to do with her and me. No, it solely had to do with the information she was given.

"Tell me, Bree, what was it that pushed you over the edge the most—your mother lying to you or me killing John?" It was a low blow, and if I were to cringe, even the slightest bit, she would call my bluff, but it was the only way I knew how to get her to acknowledge it all. She squirmed beneath me, trying to run I assumed.

"How could you even bring that up, you sick bastard?"

"Or maybe it was the lies. We all know there are tons and tons of lies. Your whole life was a giant lie. No answers were ever given. How's that feel?" I sneered.

Her fists pounded against my chest, and her legs tried every move possible to get me off her, but I wouldn't allow her to run from this anymore.

"Learn to acknowledge the hurt and pains in your life, Bree. At least you can fucking feel them. At least your heart is still beating. DEAL WITH IT!" I all but screamed at her. Her hits became more powerful, and as I pushed more weight on her, I could hear her cries growing louder.

"She lied. She fucking lied to me. No one gave me answers. No one cared, and now I have no one." She huffed out her words.

"So she fucking lied. What do you want to do about it?" I growled in her ear.

"I want to hate her. I want to know why she lied. One note is meant to make up for close to twenty years of lies."

"It's a note, Bree, not your life story. I know you want answers, but there are none to be found." My tongue darted out, licking a path directly to her ear. She tasted like cinnamon and sugar. My mouth began to salivate.

"I want revenge, I want madness and chaos. I want people to pay." She snarled every word with a demand.

"Revenge only gets you so far. Killing John didn't make me feel any better, Bree. It's a temporary feeling really. It's a false sense that maybe—just maybe, it will make you feel better to get even. Maybe it will bring back the person you lost—but it doesn't. It makes you feel worse because you inflicted the same type of pain on someone else. Yes, John deserved to die, but not by my hands."

"Death was still yapping at his footsteps, you just helped him along."

"Stop this. This isn't you. Don't let this shit consume you. Deal with it."

"I hate you. I hate everyone. I can't handle this!" she barked, her chest rumbling with my own.

"You hate me?" I questioned.

"Yes, I hate you," she roared.

"Good," I said, pressing my lips against her firmly. She bit at them so hard I could feel the skin break. Blood seeped out of the wound and onto both our lips, but I didn't care. I still wanted her. I wanted her to feel something more than what she was experiencing.

Her fists turned into grabby hands real fast as she pawed at my shirt.

"You want my cock? You want to take your frustrations out on me? Then show me, tell me what you want, *Piccolo*..." I purred against her skin. She whimpered, turning her face away from mine.

"Make me forget," she begged. Make her forget? There was no forgetting. She needed to know it.

"There is no forgetting, Bree. It is dealing and then not dealing. I refuse to allow you not to deal—so you will deal." Licking away the salty tears from her cheek, I smirked.

"But I can make you remember. I can make you remember why you're alive. I can make you heal. I can bring you to the crossroads, Bree, but you have to be the one to walk across."

"You hurt me, you fucking broke me. You think John was a monster, but you're no better. You hit me just like he hit my mother. If anything, you're the same." She sneered. Fuck! She was right, I was no better a person than John, but I loved her. I loved her with my whole heart and the difference was John had used her. I hadn't. I never would.

"You have to know I never meant to hurt you. I'm sorry, Bree. I am so fucking sorry! Do you think I will forget? Because I won't. I will never forget the night in the cabin... never forget how I hurt the one person who saved my life. I fucked up. I was lost inside my head only wanting revenge." My mind drifted back to Mack... I would paint the motherfucking walls with his blood when I was done making him pay.

"I thought the one person I had finally fallen in love with betrayed me and I was hurt. All I saw was red and Mack... Mack sounded so fucking believable. I hate myself more than I have ever hated anyone for touching you in any other way than with love. DO you hear me? Understand me right now. I know I was a bastard for hitting you, and it will never happen again. No matter what the circumstance, I will never lay a hand on you again, Bree."

Her eyes told me she didn't believe me, but her body did. She melted into my hands like chocolate. She wanted me as much as I wanted her. All the shit going on between us didn't matter nearly as much as piecing *us* back together.

"I can't handle the pain anymore..." she cried out, fresh tears running down her cheeks. She was doing something other than screaming and fighting. Wrapping both my arms around her, I cradled her head against my chest, rolling us over until I held her body against my own.

"You don't have to. You don't have to..." I whispered into her hair, holding her together as she fell apart.

"I miss her. I miss my old life. I just want it all to go back to the way it was..." she pleaded as if I could make all her dreams come true. The truth of the matter was, I couldn't fix what had already been done, but I could make the future better than the past had been.

"I promise to take care of you, to make sure all your needs are met. I will make it all worth it, just stay with me. Hold onto who you are. Please."

This is who we both were and it had never been

shown to anyone. The rawest of all raw.

Kiss by kiss, I placed her back together. Our clothes were discarded, and as I mapped out every inch of her body, I could feel myself falling deeper and deeper into the hole with her.

I had never been a man of love, but I wanted her to love me, and me to love her—more than I wanted anything in the world.

"You're my everything," I said peering deeply into her eyes as I rocked into her. Sweat covered both our foreheads, and as I pushed back the hair sticking to her forehead, I knew she knew.

"I know," she cried out in shallow breaths. Our bodies were connected in ways they never had been before. It wasn't just about fucking anymore. It was making someone feel and see you for all you were. It was about emotions, and expressing them in the form of your body.

Gripping her hip with one hand, I pushed in and out slowly, savoring the feelings. The heat coming from us burned my soul so hot I thought I might die, and a beautiful death it would be.

Minutes passed as our bodies continued to push together.

"I love you…" she whispered as her pussy clenched over and over again. I couldn't stop though. I knew one time, two times—hell, I knew any number below ten would never be enough.

"I love you, too…" I panted as I placed a kiss against her cheek. I handled her with the most tenderness, something I had never done for anyone or anything.

I felt my own release coming but pushed it away, forcing myself to give her more. I wanted her to have all of me. Gritting my teeth, I felt it coming.

"Come for me, Zerro…" she said biting her lip as her walls pulled from me everything that made me who I was.

103

My head went into the curve of her neck as I shoved into her deeply one last time. I had mended us. I had sewn us back together.

"Thank you..." she whispered into my ear as I held her against my body. My eyes drifted closed as her warmth surrounded me. Maybe, just maybe, it wasn't me who had saved her, but she who had saved me.

Hours had passed. The pounding on the door pulled me from my blissful sleep. I looked over and took notice of Bree's body slick against mine and I smiled. She had given herself to me for me to make her whole again.

"We need to talk NOW!" Jared said loudly on the other side of the door. I cringed at his voice. He sounded mad, and if I knew anything, when Jared was mad, something bad had happened.

"I have to get up, *Piccolo*..." I whispered, withdrawing myself from the bed and her body. I could've stayed there all day. All she did was groan, rolling over on the other pillow. Grabbing a pair of sleep pants from the armchair, I pulled them on and slipped out of the room. As soon as I opened the door, I was met by a scowl.

"Did you think fucking her was the best idea when her father is here? AND does it even bother you we're being hunted by the fucking FBI." I rolled my eyes at him. He must not know me as well as I thought. I looked danger straight in the eyes unless it came to Bree.

"I have a plan..." I said, pushing against his chest. I respected Jared for all he had done, but to push in my face what I had and hadn't done, and to make it seem like I didn't care, made my blood boil.

"Oh, one that doesn't consist of fucking my sister into submission?" Before I could even stop myself, I reached out and gripped him by the scruff of his shirt.

"What I do with her is none of your business. She is nothing, but a liability to all of us if her head isn't in the right place. I was giving her the comfort she needed. A lot more than you've been doing." I didn't want to have to fuck Jared up, but if he put Bree down one more time...

"Enough, boys," James said from the entrance of the hall. Jared and I stared at one another, both of us on the verge of killing someone. With a shove, I released him, walking away and into the kitchen.

"I have a fucking plan. I just need to pull a couple strings, and I will have it all in order," I said over my shoulder as they followed me into the kitchen.

"Well, it better be a good fucking idea because hiding out is getting old. We have been hiding for days." He was getting antsy. It would be nothing but messy. I didn't want to drag anyone else into this mess as it was. Jared wouldn't be the one to put the bullet in Mack's head though.

"It is... It involves a very old friend of mine..." I said pouring the coffee into a mug. I turned around, placing my cup on the table and was greeted with scowls on both faces.

"An old friend? Let's hope it is someone worth trusting...?" Jared admitted. I was sure he was confused.

Smirking, I said.... "I'm sure we can trust Devon."

chapter ten

Mack

"They killed John," Miller said as I pushed the slut off my body. Fuck. This was bad and good news. It meant one last person to deal with when this was all over, but it also meant the one thing we had to use against Bree was gone.

"Anything else?" I asked, slicking my hair back. Miller looked nervously around the room before meeting my gaze.

"Well, tell me, boy…"

"Devon and Bree got into a scuffle and she ended up running."

"Running?" I questioned moving from the bed, gripping him by the shoulders.

Yes, sir." Fuck. Devon and Miller were the two I had in the cave. They dealt with the little bitch so I wouldn't have to. I couldn't rely on these fucking people to do anything.

"And no one thought it was a good idea to tell me until now," I growled. Releasing him, I turned around scanning the room for my jeans. Picking them up off the floor, I pulled them on and walked out of the room leaving Miller to hurry behind me.

"We already moved everything. You just told us not to notify you of anything unless there were major changes," Miller stated.

Wringing my hands through my hair, I sat on one of the flimsy fucking chairs. This safe house was no good.

"We need to kill him. We need to kill all of them. If

106

they get caught by the FBI, there will be no way to kill them." At first, I was okay with Zerro getting years and years in prison, but now I was starting to think him being ten feet below my feet would be better. He deserved to be spat on.

"Where is Devon?" I asked, lighting a cigarette. I needed something to keep from wrapping my hands around these men's necks.

"Right here, sir," Devon's voice sounded as he stepped into the small cabin. His eye was slightly black, and his lip was bleeding. Bitch had done a number on him. The biggest question was why the fuck did they let her out.

"Looks like the bitch did quite a number on you." I smiled, blowing smoke out of my mouth.

"Yeah… kind of…" he commented, his eyes never leaving mine. He was one of the honest ones, so why the fuck had he done this. He used to work for Zerro before he was removed from the team and put in isolation. I stayed in touch with him for the moment when I knew I would take over. I just never planned on an actual distraction coming into the picture.

"Why was she out of the hole to begin with?" I demanded.

"I just wanted to rough her a bit. I wanted to fuck with her head. Plus, you know most of us men hadn't had any company in a while…" Devon trailed off. I got what he was saying, but it didn't mean it was okay.

"You fucking disobeyed my orders. John's dead now. Bree is gone, probably back with Zerro, and you stupid fucks are responsible for it."

"We didn't—" Miller tried to say, but I reached out wrapping my hand around his throat.

"You didn't what? It would be best if you treaded lightly with your next words because I'm about five seconds away from plunging my knife into your heart," I said blowing smoke into his face.

"Sir, it was my fault. I had gotten her out of the hole. I hadn't intended her to sucker punch me and running for her life," Devon confessed. I narrowed my eyes at him, releasing Miller with a shove.

"Then you'll be the one to get her back. You'll be the one to bring the bitch to me so I can bring the *King* to his fucking knees," I spat. I despised the man. For years, I had been his right-hand man, never receiving a thank you for half the shit I had done. Instead, I was always beaten into the ground.

He had everything while I had nothing. It would stop now. I was tired of being the fucking dirt beneath his feet. I would take every last thing from him. His home and empire had already been destroyed. But we both knew that's not what made him breathe. No, it was the girl. She had gotten into the dark part of his mind, and shined light on it. I would take her, destroy him for who he was, and then kill both of them. There was no war. There was simply a winner and a loser. They would lose…

Bree

"You're going to take her out on a fucking date with death knocking on our doorstep," Jared bellowed at Zerro. Three days had passed since I had gone off the rails and become a crazed person. Zerro had twice talked me off the cliff I was on, bringing me back to the realization there were people out there who needed to pay for all the damage they had caused.

John was dead, and though it hurt me, he was working with Mack. He had used me, and there wouldn't have been any other way around it. It was either kill or be killed, and I refused to die.

"I talked to Devon and we deciphered a plan…" Zerro said smugly. Devon had actually turned out to be the green-eyed man who freed me. He still had yet to tell any of us about this plan, but I trusted him. In a way, it was better I didn't know what we were going into until the last second.

"Zerro, secrets destroy people. Tell us this plan you have come up with," my father James said from across the living room. I was simply trying to get back to regular life by catching up on some of my favorite TV shows.

"The plan is simple. Devon is working with Mack. He used to be one of my best men. He had Intel into the FBI. I need him on my side when all this ends."

"What does that even mean?" I asked, trying to keep my attention on *The 100*. My attention slipped as I felt Zerro's gaze on me. He looked like someone had pissed in his Cheerios.

"Why the fuck are all of you second guessing me?" he growled. His hand gripped the back of the couch.

"Maybe because you have yet to tell us about the plan you say is going to save us all from life in prison," Jared threw in before I could say anything.

"You're really starting to piss me the fu—"

"Would you all just shhh… I'm really trying to watch this…" I interrupted Zerro knowing he would take his aggression out on me this evening.

"Shut up and listen to me. We need to know the plan, Zerro. You're not alone in your decisions anymore. What you do affects us all and we have the right to know." My father, the logical one, finally stepped in.

I paused the DVR and turned around to look at all three men who were shooting daggers at one another.

"Maybe they wouldn't be giving you so much flack about us going on this 'normal' date if you actually told them what the hell was going on?"

"*Piccolo*—" Zerro started.

"No, don't *Piccolo* me… Just fucking talk." Somehow, through all of this, I had found the backbone I desperately needed.

"I will put you over my knee if you…" I smiled and kind of rolled my eyes at the very thought.

"Tell us now," Jared demanded.

Sighing, he looked between all of us as if he knew there was no getting out of the mess he had caused. "Devon is the one who let Bree go. He owed me something and it was his return. He works hand in hand with Mack. Devon has a plan. He has to bring Bree to Mack—"

"Not going to happen…" James butted in. I agreed. I wanted nothing to do with the sick fuck. Not unless it meant I could put a bullet in his head.

"Let me finish. He's going to protect her at all costs… I was against it too, but I'm going to meet up with him tonight. He's going to meet Bree, and then from there, we will finish out any loose ends…"

"You're putting her in the line of death, Zerro. You know how fucked up that is?" Jared seethed. I had never seen him so angry.

"She can handle it," Zerro said shooting me a smile. I just stared at all of them. Did they realize I was sitting right here?

"Wow…" Jared yelled, throwing his hands in the air clearly frustrated. "I bet she can handle it. Look at how she handled everything else."

"Hey, now, asshole," I growled at him. James started laughing, a joyful smile crossing his face.

"Well, it's true…" he asserted.

"I was dealing with death and hurt the best way I know how. You're lucky any of you are still alive." I wouldn't have killed them, but I was pretty close to wanting to hurt someone in my rage.

Zerro laughed gruffly. "Quiet. You're merely a kitten with claws. The worst you would do is leave paper cut scratches."

Glaring, I stood. "I can make my own choices. I will do whatever is needed to kill the fucker for all the problems and heartache he has caused."

"I don't think that's a good idea, sweetie. We just got you back—" James added.

"Dad." The word sounded foreign against my tongue reminding me just how knew all this was. "I admire the fact you want to step up, but this has to be done. Mack wants me, he's gonna get me. You guys will be there if anything goes wrong. Don't worry."

"Worry..." Jared snorted. "Worrying isn't even the word I would use, Bree." I was seriously ready to pull out a knife and shank him. He had been using the big brother card a lot lately.

"She'll be fine. I trust Devon," Zerro professed.

"You trust Devon even though he's been working with Mack. That's a load of shit if I ever heard one. It's a trap, Zerro. A big fat trap and you're going to walk right into it."

I trusted Zerro. He had fucked up and done some really strange shit, but he did what was best for all of us. He pulled the trigger when he knew none of us could. I respected him for it.

"What is your plan then, Jared?" I asked, keeping my voice firm. No one had thought of anything else to do, and I was tired of hiding. I was tired of dealing with all of this shit. I wanted to be free, without wondering if I would be taken down by a gunman.

His jaw clenched as he looked at our father and me.

"We don't want to lose you, Bree. I get it's not that big of a deal, but there have to be other ways to do this." Was there another way? Would we be able to get the answers we would need? I didn't think there was another way.

"Devon worked undercover for me. He picked up the job for extra cash from Mack. He knew about Bree and me. Word with my family gets around fast, and when he found out Mack had taken Bree... well, he knew what was up. He returned her to me, knowing if he didn't, I would kill him," Zerro said unremorsefully.

That explained the connection and why he let me go without a single confrontation. He made it seem like it was his job, and when he smiled, I almost thought Zerro had put him up to it. I honestly wouldn't put it past him, but now I understood.

"So, because, you know this guy and trusted him and he released her once, you think he's going to do so again, PLUS protect her with his life?" Jared sounded unbelieving and James looked like he was about ready to punch something. This wasn't going very well.

"I can take care of myself, guys…" No one looked at me, or even acknowledged what I had said. Fucking men. This was typical of them.

"It doesn't matter if you can take care of yourself, you shouldn't have to," Zerro said sternly as if he were talking to a misbehaving child.

"Well, I can, and I will." There was no fighting about this. I would do what needed to be done to put all this shit behind us.

"Devon will do all he can to protect Bree. She was unharmed the first time around."

"Yeah, because John was still alive." Jared reminded him. At the mention of John's name, a massive hole formed in my chest. I wasn't sure I would ever get over what he had done to Mom, but I knew I would never forget what he did to me.

"I agree with Jared on this. John being alive helped immensely." Thinking back on my time spent in the cave, I'm sure my treatment would've been far worse if John had already been dead. No matter how much I hate to admit it, in a way, he kept me alive. Even Devon had treated me cruel, but through it all, he never hurt me. He might have messed with my emotions, but he never laid a hand on me.

"Well, Mack knows John is dead," Zerro said, frustrated with all of us, I was certain.

"Let's meet this Devon guy before we allow her to go with him willingly. Plus, isn't Mack going to say something if she isn't roughed up a bit? What about Devon? There has to be an apparent struggle. It has to look real," James commented. Ugh. All this talk about death was starting to depress me.

"We'll figure it out later. The plan is Bree and I meet up with Devon before we go out. Talk to him. Pretend all is normal, and in about a week, Devon comes and gets her. I'll kick his ass and scruff him up a bit," Zerro commanded.

"Whatever, but if she gets hurt… it's on you." Jared all but scoffed, pushing past Zerro. As the room settled, I stared at him, waiting for whatever it was he would say.

"Just know I will not let anyone spill your blood." There was so much determination in his eyes it almost frightened me.

"I know. You don't have to tell me," I responded, stepping up onto my tiptoes so I could place a kiss on his lips.

"Good," he said. There was a faraway look in his eyes. Whatever he was thinking wasn't good. Not for any of us.

The afternoon passed with breeze as I sat on the couch and vegged out with James, and Jared. Zerro was absent for some time before coming out of our bedroom. There was a time when someone needed to be alone. I had been there, done that. I understood the need.

"Thank God! Tell Bree to stop making us watch this extremely distasteful TV drama," Jared shouted to Zerro, smiling at me. Jerk.

"Hey, fuckface, it's a hit TV show. Tell us what you created that's a hit TV show," I said shooting him a dirty look before directing my attention back to the screen.

"He didn't create nothing, but I did…" James said, laughing gruffly. What was he talking about?

"Good one, Dad," Jared said, laughing. Then it hit

me… He created Jared and me. Well, kind of created us.

"Good joke, James," Zerro said coming to sit down next to me. He had a Pepsi in hand, obviously knowing I needed some caffeine. I took the drink from him curious as to what was weighing on his mind.

"Everything okay?" I asked softly, hoping no one else had heard. Keeping his lips sealed tightly, he gave me a curt nod.

"Can we please watch Dallas Cowboy's Cheerleaders or even Football? Hell, I would rather watch Food Network," Jared complained, which in turn caused me to chuck the remote controller at his head.

"Thank you…" he responded loutishly at me.

"Are you going to be ready to go soon?" Zerro whispered into my hair, one of his hands landing on mine. His skin caused mine to tingle, and the last thing I could think about was he and I going out on a date. I simply wanted him to take me back to the bedroom. Call me fucking crazy, but with all the pain, death, and hate surrounding us, being close to someone made it so much easier to get through.

"Uh, of course. When do you want to leave?" I asked. Zerro had changed so much. He went from being a man who was dark with more secrets than anyone else had to a man I loved. Even though those secrets still lingered, and sometimes I couldn't decipher his next move, I knew he loved me.

"How about…." he said pondering…. "Now?" he questioned with an eyebrow raised.

"Whenever you want, Mr. King…" I giggled. Leaning real close into my face, his nose brushing against mine, he said, "If I'm the King, then you're the Queen."

The very words left me breathless reminding me of why I loved him so much. He might be a monster, but he was my monster.

chapter twelve

Mack

"When are they going to come out of hiding? They can't fucking hide forever," I yelled throwing my phone against the mattress. I had been hiding out in this drab fucking cabin instead of the lavish mansion soon to be mine.

"I'm not sure they're alone. That's all I know, sir," Miller added like he was some smart shit or something. He needed to keep his mouth shut before he found himself swimming with the fishes.

"No fucking way. Did you want a prize for stating the obvious?" I growled reaching across the table for his throat. I was angry and impatient. If blood wasn't shed soon... I would start killing my own men until I could go out and do the job myself.

"Sir...." Miller sounded scared. He had a reason to be, but then again, why was some pussy like him working for me.

"Miller...." I yelled anger radiating from me.

"Calm down, sir." Devon's voice vibrated through my mind.

"Do you have any new info?" I growled turning my aggression to him. He looked like a kid... hardly old enough to be chasing after people like Alzerro, who would kill him on site?

"I think I have an idea of where they're staying. I'm going to go scope it out this evening." His voice never wavered, and his eyes stayed on mine. He wasn't lying.

"Good and you best bring back something to tell

me. I'm going crazy sitting here waiting."

"Sir, we could be shooting or throwing knives..." Miller added. Ahhh, yes we could be.

A Texas-size grin showed on my face. "You're right, we could. Get my knives, Devon," I ordered. I had some aggression I needed to work out, and Miller reminding me of ways to do so only made my life easier. Devon scurried out of the room to retrieve the knives and I stared at Miller.

"You know, while I worked for Alzerro, he was very keen on making sure nothing, and I do mean nothing, scared the men who worked for him...."

Miller nodded as if he was acknowledging what I had said, but the sweat forming on his forehead, and the faraway look in his eyes told me he wasn't anywhere but here in this room with me.

"Do you have any fears, Miller?" I asked my voice menacing. What a pussy! He was shaking like a leaf in the wind. Where had John found these men?

"No, sir." He sounded determined, but one look at him said he was lying.

"Good. Go stand against the far wall. We're going to test this theory out." Devon placed a knife in my hand. It was light weight and the blade glistened in the light. The need to sink it into flesh was overwhelming. I could just imagine the blood dripping from the blade as I sunk blade after blade int—

"Sir," Devon asked, concern clearly found in his voice.

"What?" I questioned with raised eyebrows. If I had no way of getting my hands on Bree and Alzerro, then I would do with what I did have—Miller.

"What are you doing, sir?" Devon questioned once again.

"Never question me, or it will be you who is on the receiving end of this knife," I growled gripping the end of the knife with so much anger, I was certain I would break it. My words weren't a threat—they were a promise.

Devon said nothing, his eyes simply widening as he took in the scene before him. Turning my attention back to the coward, I narrowed my eyes with precision. Where would he bleed the most?

My mind drifted back to the very first time Zerro had ever asked me that question.

"MACK. When I tell you to do something, you do it. There is no reason to fear these small things. Death is always following these people." He all but yelled at me. I *was only nineteen. He had been killing for years, and this... this was my very first time.*

I hadn't landed the knife right, so the person was struggling. Their death would be painful.

"He's hurting though..." I tried to say. I wasn't a *child, but watching someone bleed to death... It did something to your heart. It pulled the strings tight and made it beat fast.*

"What's your point? He deserved to die? What are you scared of?" Was it a trick question?

"Nothing, sir," I immediately answered him. I didn't *want to be the next one with a knife in my neck.*

"Good, because being scared is a weakness. You're to be afraid of nothing, not a fucking thing, when you're in my kingdom. Do you understand?" he questioned. I nodded *my head as I watched him lift his foot. What was he doing?*

Then I heard the crunching of bones, the splatter of brain matter, and blood against the ground.

"This is what we do to people who are weak... scared," he snarled, staring down at what was left of the *man's body. I never even got the man's name.*

Pulling myself back to the present, I stared at the man before me. He was weak. He was scared.

With complete control, I arched my arm back and threw the knife. It flew through the air, barreling toward Miller. His eyes grew large, and I could practically hear his heart beat from where I stood as the knife sunk into the deep word directly above his head. He wasn't just a coward—he was a liar, too. He wasn't just scared—no, he was fucking terrified.

"You're a liar…" I spat the words with venom. "You said you were scared of nothing, but it is clear to me as I watch you shake in your fucking skin, you are in fact scared of something…" I smiled, because I was a fucker like that. Nothing got me harder than making people pay for what they did wrong. I recognized failure.

"Sir, give him a break. He just started with us—" Devon tried to cut in. I turned glaring at him. He was lucky I needed him. He had the information I needed. Killing him would be a grave mistake at his time. His death would have to wait until later.

"Breaks are for the fucking weak…" Taking a deep breath, I smiled before I threw the next knife. It landed just millimeters from his throat. Hmmm…. his throat… yes, that's where the next one would land.

"Are you going to beg?" I mocked. At the very least, he could go out feeling like a man. If I had one thing to thank Alzerro for it was his ruthless ways. He had taught me any emotion outside of killing was unneeded. When I put the bullet in his head and fucked Bree, it would be from his teachings.

"Men don't beg," he said quietly. His voice was wobbly. Was he going to cry? Was this fucking pathetic excuse for a human going to cry? I had seen women handle death better than this excuse.

"Glad you figured it out," I mocked, gripping the blade in my hand. With one single arch, I whipped the blade at him, watching his eyes dilate, and his chest move for the last time. The blade sank straight into his throat, and I listened to the gurgling sound of him struggling to breathe while blood filled his throat. As I watched the light leave his eyes, a sick sadistic smile spread across my lips causing my heart to swell with happiness. "You didn't have to kill him." Devon sounded as if he was actually hurt.

"Yes, I did. He was a weakness. He wouldn't have done anything but drag us down." I was satisfied with all I had done, and as I watched the blood pour from him... I smiled even more. Blood wasn't a sign of death, but a sign of victory. I had won—they just didn't know it yet.

"Remove his body and get ready to go. We have a plan to follow through with." I was going to get them. Both of them, even if I had to die fucking trying.

Inevitable

chapter thirteen

Zerro

I watched her fidget with the hem of her shirt. Was she nervous? I hadn't been myself lately. I had lost the roughness in my words and touch. I wasn't the same man as I was before.

"This is... well... a very domesticated version of you..." Bree laughed easily, her hair moving as small breaths came from her mouth. We hadn't discussed anything pertaining to her being taken because I wanted this date to be just that—a date. A normal thing two people would do when they wanted to get to know more about one another.

Dating wasn't really my thing. I never fucked and stayed. Hell, I never even comforted anyone until Bree. I didn't know what compassion, love, or softness was. Death, rage, and fury were all I knew. She lit a spark in my cold heart-stirring flames not stirred since my mother had died.

"See, I can do shit without a gun." I smirked, reaching for my glass of water. We were eating at a simple diner here in town. The place reminded me of one of those towns you would see in movies. Everyone had immaculate lawns, two and half kids, and a wraparound fence in the back yard. The crime rate was low, and everyone played a part in the community.

This wasn't my kind of scene. Hell, being normal wasn't my kind of fucking thing at all. It felt strange, but at the same time, it felt welcoming.

"Lies…" She hissed out, taking the straw of her drink in between her teeth. "I bet you have your gun right in your back. I bet you keep looking around the room to see who the first person will be to get shot if shit goes wrong, and I bet, more than anything, being this domesticated is fucking with your head."

Did I really have it written all over my face or was she just starting to know me for who I was?

"Dear Bree," I growled reaching across the table to grip her chin, "you know far more than anyone." Had I known taking her from that shabby farmhouse months prior would cost me everything, would I have done it? Even for love? Probably not. Life had a fucked up way of twisting things, even when we didn't want something to happen.

Letting the straw slip from her mouth, she bit her bottom lip, which in turn caused my cock to swell. She made me want to fuck her a hundred different ways.

"Your double bacon cheeseburger…" the waitress said, a slight annoyance to her tone as she slid Bree's plate in front of her.

"And an omelet for you..." She all but shoved the plate in front of me. Anger simmered deep within me. What was this bitch's problem, and why did she feel the need to all but shove my food at me?

"Excuse me, but is there a problem?" I growled pushing the plate forward. I caught Bree's eyes as apprehension showed in them. She didn't want a blowout, and neither did I, but no one gets away with treating my girl or me like shit.

"Problem…." Was she pondering if there was a problem or not? She had five fucking seconds to tell me if there was, and what it was?

"Yeah, you know like, an issue. There isn't a damn reason to shove shit at me. There is most definitely no reason to take that tone with my woman, and if you care about your job in the least bit, you'll take the high fucking road."

"Zerro…" Bree said quietly…

"No. It's not okay to be disrespectful."

"Honey, you need to get your dog on a fucking leash." The waitress, whose name I didn't get, walked away.

"Bitch…" I was this close to reaching for my fucking gun and placing a bullet in her head. Guess Pleasant Fucking Villes crime rate would go up to one with me around.

"You need to relax, Zerro. This is the real world. There are no Mafia people here. That's all kind of made for the movies, so while we both have to learn to adjust to shit, you can't just go around ordering people around and pulling your gun out." Bree all but scolded me as if I were a child.

"I didn't pull my gun out," I said slipping a piece of the omelet into my mouth. It didn't taste like my cook's cooking, but then again, not a lot of food did.

Arching an eyebrow, she watched me. "Really, so when I watched your hand slip into your back it wasn't just to grab your wallet so you could leave a nice tip?" Was she mocking me?

"I will have you know, I can fucking get my gun out whenever I want."

Snorting, she glared. "You act like I'm taking a piece of your manhood or something?" She was—my gun was the closest thing to my home I had left.

"It's my gun and if I want to put a bullet in her head, I will." I took another bite of my food, and then a drink of water, waiting for her to eat her own food.

Shaking her head, she turned her attention to something out the window. "And to think I actually thought maybe you were changing. Thinking maybe you had left behind the murderous person I had met months ago."

Desperately, I wanted to tell her I had—I had let the person go I once was when I shot John, but the truth was I hadn't. I had covered him up. I had pushed a part of me to the bottom... but there was no changing that part of me. It would always be there.

Leaning in, to the point where I was leaning onto the table, I said, "If you thought that part of me was gone, you're naïve. I was born into this life, Bree. I will never allow that part of me to go away. It's been ingrained into me since the start of life. If I had a choice, believe me when I say I would've made one."

I could all but feel the sadness seep into both of us. There was an ocean forming between us. I thought I had actually saved her, brought her out of the dark, but maybe it was me who was still keeping her in the dark. Maybe I was what was hurting her the most.

"Everyone has a choice, Zerro. Everyone has a chance to change things for the better. Your past doesn't define you and without a future path outlined, you're free to do whatever you want."

What was she saying? I was growing angry from simple confusion. Her words were always littered with riddles. Some I understood and others, I didn't.

"There is no path to choose from, Bree. No path to walk along. My path was chosen long before you came along."

Tears formed behind her eyes, and I knew I had struck some kind of nerve. I was confused though and hurt. How could I change something where I never had a choice? How the fuck did we even get to this subject. We were supposed to be having a simple dinner? Just like normal people did.

J.L. Beck

"I didn't me—"

"No, you did. The Mafia will always run in your blood and I get that. I seriously fucking do. You've lost so much and dealt with so much pain, I knew it wouldn't be easy to get over. Just know, the person who raised me from birth died at your hands and I had to learn to deal with my anger elsewhere...."

"What the fuck are you talking about?" I barked drawing attention to us. I didn't care though. I had no idea what she meant by that statement.

"You need to get over whatever is inside of you holding you back from moving on. I know you watched your mom die, but I watched you kill John. Looks like we aren't far from one another, after all."

Still reeling from her words, lost in my own mind, I didn't even realize she had gotten up to leave. Where did she think she was going?

I gripped the table to the point of pain and pushed myself up, throwing a fifty down before I walked out in search of her.

As soon as I was out the door, I ran to her, grabbing her by the lapels of her coat. I turned her to face me. Her cheeks were streaked with fresh tears.

"You want to tell me what the fuck is going on because I'm confused here." Frustrated with the whole situation, I started rubbing my palm against my head. I didn't know how to talk about problems. I simply dealt with them in a different manner.

"There is nothing to talk about, Zerro. You are who you are, and I made a mistake thinking you had changed."

"Changed? What the hell would make you think I had changed?" Had I really lost my touch? Had being out of the world I had grown up in pushed me to grow soft, and if so, was I hurting her more by dragging her down a confusing path.

"You..." She shoved against my chest with far more

127

strength than I knew she had, "you're just so dumb. You don't even absorb anything…" Frustration laced her words, and I wasn't sure if I should talk or not.

"I thought you changed for us. For some reason, I thought when all this was over, we would be able to be together. I thought maybe you would leave the Mafia." She seemed surprised by her own confession, and my own heart started to beat out of control. I was shocked into silence.

"I—" What was I supposed to say to that? I couldn't ever just walk away from the Mafia. This wasn't a fucking career choice and the fact she made it seem like it made me angry.

"You think this is what I want? You think I want to be this person? You think I want to drag your feelings all over the place and kill people. Hell, I'm killing myself in the process, Bree…" I huffed the words out, every single word a lash meant to be against her skin. I wanted to hurt her, shake her to death. Make her realize I couldn't choose between her and the Mafia.

"I thought—I mean—couldn't we have—" Her words weren't making sense.

"No, we couldn't. There was no happy ever after for us, Bree. I planned on winning this war and where I went from there, I didn't know."

Her face grew red with every word I said, and I felt my chest cavity breaking in two. My heart was bleeding for her and for the future we may or may not have.

"I never asked for a happily ever after, Zerro." She shoved against my chest getting in my face.

"I simply wanted to know what your intentions were. Why after everything had happened, you would want to stay doing this? This isn't you."

What she was saying was causing me to think. To think about things I couldn't. This was the road I was meant to travel.

"It is me. This is me. The monster in the flesh

before you. Right in sight." I pushed her back until she was against a wall with nowhere to run. The man I used to be was right under the surface. The man who would have wiped the alley with her face. The man who would've fucked her and then threw her to his men. Was I still that man?

"This isn't you." She fought back. "This is the shell of a man who was used to existing simply because dealing with the pain of what happened had been too much. Think whatever you want, Alzerro King, but know you can't hide who you really are. I've already had a taste of the man underneath, and I will do anything I can to never let him go." Was she delirious? I had just told her the monster I was, and still, she stood before me as if she thought she could save me.

"There isn't any saving me, Bree. There is no stopping whatever will happen from happening. I helped you through your loss because it was my fault It was my jo—""

"Just shut up already." She interrupted me stunning me into silence once more. I gritted my teeth so hard I was afraid my jaw would shatter.

"It's my fault your mother's dead. So why not hate me, too? Why not fucking ruin it all because you can't move on." She was seething, but the tears were there trailing down her cheek. I had caused this destruction. I knew I would break her, hurt her, and yet still, I tried. I tried to be so much more than what I was.

"I don't know what to say…" I muttered astounded at her behavior and how the night's events had played out.

"Nothing. Say nothing because when this is all over, I will be the one to walk away from you, not the other way around." And then she was running, she was leaving me, and I felt the walls closing around who I was. Around everything that had happened between us.

The debt was settled, but our future was inevitable.

We were born to enemies none the less.

chapter fourteen

Bree

I was so fucking stupid. I was running from him, and by the sound of silence surrounding me, I knew he wasn't following me. Maybe he didn't care, maybe none of it mattered, but I knew if I couldn't save him from his own mind, no one could. I had dealt with so much in the last week. I had learned my mom had an affair, and James, Jared's father was my own, and who I thought was my father had secretly been working with the FBI. He had been using me as a pawn in his own personal game.

"Why the fuck do I even care?" I growled to myself, falling to my knees in the park. I had run for what seemed like forever, but really hadn't been more than ten minutes.

As I sunk further into the ground, I wonder why I was even trying. Why, right this second, I didn't call Jared and tell him to take me as far away as he could and hide me. He had asked, one time late at night. He had said he would do anything he could to contain the sliver of happiness he had.

"You know someone like you, out in a park like

this—not really all that safe." A deep voice rumbled behind me. I turned around, staring into a pair of deep green, vibrant eyes. I knew those eyes, the voice, and it did nothing to stop the sickness in my stomach from bubbling over.

"Who cares what is safe anymore." I was stupid— so fucking stupid. I knew it, and Devon knew it, too. Maybe that's why he was here. Maybe Zerro had called him to fetch me.

"Obviously, not you. There's a basket case fucking man searching the hills for you and you're running in the park alone." His hair was a little too long for my liking, and his eyes—those eyes peered deep into my soul. It was as if you couldn't lie to him to save your very own life.

"After all I went through, I almost want to fucking give up and turn myself in. Have you ever just been tired of running?" I asked not really sure why I was asking. I didn't even know why he was still standing here talking to me. He wasn't my keeper.

Squatting down on his heels, he looked me straight in the eyes. "I live a double life, Bree. I'm pretty sure I have thought about running more than you ever have in your entire life."

"Then why don't you?" I asked naïve to the understanding. People always had a choice, right?

He smiled, and it wasn't a genuine kind, but more of a comforting one. "There is no point in running. If I ran, I would be running forever, and what fun would that be? I wouldn't get much sleep at night having to look over my shoulder at every corner."

The wind picked up, pushing my hair into my face. I had no reason not to believe what he was saying. It made sense. Running was the same as sitting and waiting. Both caused a knot of anxiety to form in your belly. I guess all I really wanted was freedom.

"Did he send you to fetch me?" I growled, changing

the subject. I would be fifty shades of fucking angry if he did. I wasn't a dog.

"No. He doesn't even know I'm with you right now." His voice was calm, but something about the fact Zerro didn't know sent shivers down my spine. I couldn't tell if Devon was the good guy or the bad?

"Why not?"

"He didn't need to know. After all, he is the one who let you go," Devon said stating the obvious. Had he been watching us?

"Who are you, and what is your plan in all of this?" My voice turned high pitched, terror was filling my mind. Running wasn't a good idea, after all.

"My plan hasn't changed. I'm not here to kill you or hurt you so calm down. I can practically hear your heartbeat through your jacket." A sliver of amusement showed on his face calming my nerves slowly.

Coming to a stand, I dusted off the leaves and headed for a nearby bench. I wasn't ready to go back to Zerro yet—if he was even waiting for me.

"Zerro told me you had a plan. You guys were devising some shit behind everyone's backs." The way I said it made it seems as if he was deceiving all of us.

"Wow, the asshole really can keep a secret…" Devon laughed loud and proud. The creases on his face told me he didn't often smile, which was a shame.

"Hardly, we got it out of him anyway," I remarked. A moment of silence passed between us as the wind rustled the leaves in the trees.

"Figures…."

"Why are you here then?"

Shrugging his shoulders, he pulled a knife out of his pocket. I gasped, and my first reaction was to run.

"Shhh," he said, placing his hand on my knee in a reassuring gesture. "I just watched Mack kill someone. He killed someone for no fucking reason, simply because he could. Do you know how disgusting that is to me?" His words sneered together. His hold on the blade became intense.

"I can imagine it would be extremely unpleasant and completely disgusting." My tone was all matter of fact, as my heart rattled in my chest. This man was going to give me a fucking heart attack.

"You know, I never wanted to hurt you. I never would've. They made us put you in the hole. John made us fucking do it to you. A man I personally worked with, Bree. I worked with John for a couple years, Bree. He was after answers, and all he had to do was discover my secret…"

"What secret?" I asked curiously. I wanted to know what had happened.

"I worked for Alzerro the whole time. I was one of his men before I became part of the FBI. I promised him I would let him know shit from the inside and eventually, we parted ways. I did my own thing and he did his."

"He mentioned something about you working for him. That explains why you let me go. Didn't want your ass kicked, huh?" I joked.

"No, I really just wanted to let you go. I hoped you would run instead of seeking answers. It kind of sucks to find out shit you wish you hadn't."

"You talk as if you have experience with this kind of thing." As we talked more, I felt myself melting into the bench. It had been months since I talked to someone on the outside.

"You have no clue. I needed money so I volunteered to do a job for Mack. Little did I know it was way more than a fucking job…" His body shifted as he stared up at the sky. For an FBI agent, he seemed like he was at his wits ends.

"Welcome to my world. I've been in hiding for months now. Pushed and shoved around. Secrets have been thrown my way, and somehow, I'm still breathing…" The air shuffled past us, and I took in a big gulp.

"You know I should be really fucking mad at you." I laughed nudging him in the side. His eyes came down to meet my own, and my breath caught for a mere second. Was I attracted to him, or was it the fact I was still extremely pissed at Alzerro.

"Hey, now, I had to do what I had to do. Blowing my cover would've meant a bullet in both of our heads." He was right—blowing his cover would've been the end of all of this. I probably wouldn't have ever found out the truth.

"Point made. But if you ever throw a bucket of water on me again, I'm stabbing you in the chest." I wasn't joking.

"Are you waiting for him to come and get you, or do you want to come with me?" Devon asked as he changed the subject. He slipped a smile somehow into his words. I wasn't sure if I should leave the park with him. What if he took me to Mack before it was time? Then again, going back to Jared's and sitting in the same room was no fun either. I didn't want to listen to Zerro tell me all the things he couldn't do.

Crossing my arms over my chest, I looked at him in a defensive manner. "I'm not waiting for him to come get me. I will go with you, but I want to make sure you aren't taking me to Mack yet."

Zerro would call me stupid, insane, illogical. I knew what I was doing was wrong, but he needed to be worried. He needed to freak out, to realize anything could happen.

Smirking at me, he laughed. His whole body shook, and my eyes wandered all over the place.

"I promise not to feed you to the devil just yet. I'll take you out for some drinking and have you back at home before midnight. Since I know you'll turn into a pumpkin and all." He had to be playing, right?

"Okay, let's go," I urged before Zerro came and

actually found me. The last thing I wanted to do was deal with him right now.

Sometimes, people had to make their own path, and after everything had happened between us, I was going to do just that.

"Here," Devon said tugging on my jacket as we entered the club he wanted to go. It was two towns over and though I was nervous, I was excited, too. I hadn't been able to do anything my age. The beat of the music rumbled under our feet and vibrated through our bodies making it hard to breathe.

"What?" I all but yelled—not intentionally, of course. Something cold and metal was placed in my hand, and when I looked down, I caught the glint of a knife in the strobe lights. What the hell?

"I can't tak—"

"You can, and you will. You need it in case something happens to you. I can't believe Zerro didn't give you something already."

Holding the knife in my hands, I gently slipped it into my boot without another glance. The last thing I needed was someone thinking I actually had a weapon.

"You're right… I don't understand why he hasn't given me a weapon yet…" The more it sat on my mind, the more it started to bother me. Did I still love Zerro? Yes. Did I think he would be able to adjust the changes? I didn't know. I didn't know what the future held for either of us.

"He's Alzerro. He doesn't really answer to anyone," Devon kind of joked. I say kind of because it actually seemed more like something was bothering him, deep down.

"I'm thirsty… and I want to dance," I said into his ear as I watched the couples out on the floor gyrating against one another. My eyes were mesmerized by their very movements, some I had never seen before.

"Drink first, and then maybe, if you're lucky, dancing." He winked dragging me through the deep crowd. People surrounded us on every angle. My eyes roamed over every single object.

"I need a beer, and..." He trailed off looking at me for an answer. Like I had one. I had said many times before I hardly ever drank. Any time I did, I regretted it. To be here doing this caused a ting of guilt to form in my chest. Was it okay to be moving on from things days after your supposed father's death?

"And a Malibu and Pineapple." He finished his sentence as he slammed back the beer the bartender had sat in front of him. I didn't stare at him as he did, simply because it felt wrong.

"What's that?" I hadn't heard of the drink before.

"It's a girly drink and will be perfect for someone who looks like an ounce of liquor will knock her over."

Narrowing my eyes, I whispered, "Are you making fun of me?"

"Quite possibly," he said back in a much flirtier tone. What was his antic? What was he attempting to do by all of this? Hanging around Zerro made me think everything over so much more than I should.

A drink was pushed in front of me so I took it. It looked like pineapple juice, and as I put the straw to my lips and sucked, I waited for the awful burn to come. When it didn't, and my taste buds were met with a tangy pineapple flavor, I all but sighed. It was delicious, tangy reminding me of the beach.

"Good?" he questioned his own eyes roaming over the dance floor. The club wasn't overly huge, simply a two story building with a long ass line outside.

"Very," I mumbled taking the straw between my teeth for another sip, which turned into a gulp. The pounding of the music drowned out all other thoughts, and for a moment, I slipped into another form. Someone I didn't even know. My body swayed to the fast beat of music, and all I could think of doing was getting up and grabbing someone to dance with.

"What were your real reasons for coming with me?" Devon yelled though I could barely hear him. I loved this environment. The darkness, the smell of sweat, and the smoke in the air. It was exhilarating making me forget about my past until Devon brought it up.

"First, I wanted to get away from Zerro. He's up my ass all the time and, believe it or not, it surprised me he let me run." Pausing for a moment, I took another drink completely dismissing the straw.

"Secondly, I needed out. I needed air, and I needed to see things differently." My head was getting a little fuzzy, but I still wanted to keep going. One drink wouldn't be enough for all I had been dealing with.

"You know he loves you, right?" Devon asked, but it was more all matter of fact like, the amusement leaving his voice as he took the empty glass from my hands. I wanted to say something like get me another, but I knew it would be rude.

"I know he loves me. Not like I don't. I just think if he expected me to let things of the past go, then he should, too. His mother was murdered by my father, and he killed him in cold blood. It's okay for me to have to move on, but it's not okay for him. He's been holding the grudge since like forever."

Another drink was placed in my hands, and I turned to Devon rewarding him with a smile. He was earning huge brownie points from me. Even if he had the chance of not walking tomorrow. Zerro would kill him if he knew where he brought me. I sipped my second drink a little slower and moved to the beat of the new song some more.

"I feel so close to you right now, it's a force field..."

I sang the words totally off key and had it not been for the volume of the music, everyone would've been covering their ears.

The alcohol was settling into my veins, and slowly but surely, I found myself wandering out onto the dance floor. People surrounded me in masses as our bodies moved against one another's. Nothing mattered at this moment more than spreading my wings and being free.

For the first time in months, I wasn't afraid, I wasn't ashamed—I was just me. My hair stuck to my skin as my body became encased in a shell of sweat. Then I felt him. I didn't have to see him to know he was there. My heart tugged to him. My body yearned for him. I continued to move to the beat, wondering how he had found me.

"*Piccolo…*" His sweet voice sounded like a deep ocean and had me melting like chocolate. Why was I mad at him again?

"Alzerro King…" I slurred my words but only slightly. His hands encompassed my hips as he pushed his own to meet my movements. His whole body was against mine as I moved. Our hearts beat as one as his thrusts became so much more. His length pressed firmly into my ass told me I had some kind of hold on him still.

"Ahhh…." I moaned unable to contain the pleasure claiming me.

"Believe me, I know…" he whispered against my skin as his hands roamed my body moving me to the rhythm he wanted. I was hyperaware of my clenching pussy and my need for him was almost starving.

"I'm sorry, Bree. I'm so fucking sorry I allowed you to run without following. I'm sorry you think me loving you might not be enough." I could hear the suffering in his voice. Pushing back against him, he gripped me hard. If he were sorry, he would have to prove it.

Rubbing my ass into his groin did me no good when it came to me feeding my own needs.

"Slow down, beautiful," he growled, taking my earlobe in-between his teeth. Slow down? If anything, I needed to speed up.

Whirling around so I could face him, I rubbed my hand between his legs. He was more than ready for me. He was straining against his pants, and by the look in his eyes, I could tell I was playing with fire.

"If you're truthfully sorry…. prove it." I leaned into his face whispering the words in his ear. A fire was ignited within me. As much as I wanted to be mad at Devon for giving away our location, I knew I couldn't be. He had given me this small sliver of happiness in this world of chaos… With a gift like that, I couldn't be mad.

"Oh, I will, *Piccolo*… I fucking will…" His lips found my neck, and in a flash, I was melting into a puddle of mush. My resistance to him was nothing. The bites, kisses, and sucks of my own flesh were all that could be heard. His hands skimmed over my body until they landed on my ass. With one quick movement, he had me wrapping my legs around his waist.

I didn't care we were in a club or there could be people looking at us. No. All I cared about was Zerro proving to me how sorry he was. In a matter of seconds, we were pushing through what I could assume was a back door. My back slammed against a brick wall as his mouth assaulted mine in a manner saying everything he couldn't.

Pulling away just slightly, he bit my lip causing me to groan. "If you run from me again, I will spank you until your ass cheeks glow red. Then I'll fuck you like I hate you… Got it?" He commanded my attention, and my pussy purred in appreciation. Instead of saying yes, I nodded my head, my eyes glowing with a deep need.

"Good, now release from me. I'm fucking you the way I want to." I smirked a little. I released my legs slowly, sliding down the wall. Once I found my footing, he grabbed me by the arm and pulled me into the alleyway.

"Fucking me the way you want to?" I teased him, hoping just for a smidge of the darkness in his eyes.

"The. Way. I. Fucking. Want. To." He turned growling at me, making sure I heard every single word he had said. My insides tingled with desires far darker than I had ever wanted. In this new world, life could be pulled from you in a second.

A walked next to him casually as if I wasn't walking to my impending death by fucking. Our footsteps echoed on the pavement, and around the back of the lot, we came to a stop in front of a sleek car. It said 'I have money,' and it looked like sex on wheels.

"Where did you get this?" I asked curiously as I ran my hand across the hood. My pussy clenched at the very thought of being taken against the hood of the car.

"Where I got it from doesn't matter nearly as much as what I'm going to do with you in it," he exclaimed, a dark one-sided smile crossing his face. I took one step covering the distance between us.

"Fuck me… Please…" I begged, my eyes urging him for more. The idea of doing such a taboo thing in public was exhilarating, and even though I knew we could be caught and found by Mack at any second, I still wanted him. The idea of being found just added more to it.

"Oh, I will," he growled cupping me between my jeans. My body bowed at his very touch, and as I reached up on my tiptoes, he came down to me with an intensity rivaled by nothing.

Spinning me around, I caught myself on the hood of the car. The black paint sparkled in the light. One second I was wearing pants, and the next, they were wrapped around my ankles as he pushed my panties to the side.

"Fuckkk…." I said quietly. Two fingers entered me with so much intensity, I found myself leaning against the car more and more as I slid up and down with every stroke.

"I hope you know how much I love you, *Piccolo*…"

He growled in my ear as he continued to pump in and out of me. Leaning on my forearms, I pushed against him, wanting my own release now.

"Why?" I huffed out, questioning why we were even talking at this point. All I could think about was his cock inside of me.

"Because, I'm about to fuck you like I hate you. Hold on, baby…" His words were the only warning I was given as he withdrew from me and pulled at his belt. In less than five seconds, I felt his cock probing at my entrance. My mouth watered as he slid into me all the way to the hilt.

"Oh, god…" I cried out, my head falling toward the hood of the car. I could hear the traffic on the other side of the building, and if anyone drove down the alleyway, they would see us. Except none of those things bothered me.

Slamming into me over and over again, I found myself on the very verge of coming. Skin slapping against skin echoed around me, only pushing me further and further.

"Come for me…" he growled gripping my hair tightly as he pulled my head back to meet his lips. As if on command, my pussy clenched around him as he continued to pump in and out of me.

One of his hands gripped my hip hard while the other kept my lips on his. At that moment, all I could feel or see was Alzerro King and not another fucking thing mattered when we were like this.

"Give it to me, give me all of you," he whispered his words, covering my body in a blanket of need. We were both covered in sweat, and with one shove, he was deeper than he ever had been.

"Come for me, Bree, come all over my cock…." he said tensing. His own releases were mere strokes away, and if twice wasn't good enough, I came again, my insides falling over and over again.

Releasing my hair, he flipped me over, and pulled

out, only to stare deeply into my eyes as he stroked himself. There was a deep look in his eyes, almost fear, and as he came, I watched his vision swarm with every emotion known to mankind. My own body shuddered with aftershocks as his hot cum landed on my sweat clad body.

The tension eased out of both of us, a huge smile showing on my face. The drinks I had earlier were a forgotten effect as the endorphins of my own release circulated through me.

"I love you, Bree... This will forever be a learning process for me. All I ask you to do is to try. If not for me, for us." The way he talked and looked at me had my walls of existing anger crumbling. If you really loved someone, could you stay mad at them? Sometimes you had to pick your battles...

"I will... Now take me home," I said softly, sitting up, and pulling my pants on. The wetness of his come against my skin caused me to bite my lip. I was his in every way, shape, and form.

Inevitable

Zerro

My blood boiled the second Devon had texted me telling me he was taking her to a club. He had run into her, and instead of fucking calling me right away, he took her somewhere. He gave her what I couldn't, even if it was only for a moment. *Freedom.*

I knew from the way she moved her body against mine being free of the chains of this life was exhilarating. She could breathe without restriction.

As she lay on our bed in Jared's house, my mind wandered. I wasn't lying to her when I said I wasn't sure I could be the man she wanted me to be. I had a soft side, but under it all, I didn't think I could let the harshness go. I was born this way, made this way and hardened by the harsh aspects of my life.

"You found her?" James questioned me as I took a seat in the living room. I wasn't ready to go and lay next to her. It would just make me want to fuck her into submission over and over again. Running from me was stupid, so fucking stupid.

"Yeah, I did," I mumbled my hands running through my hair. I was exhausted. The truth was though I was used to all this, all I ever had to protect was myself. Having to think about more than just myself—well, was just exhausting.

"I'm assuming from the look on your face it wasn't somewhere you expected to find her?" What was with all the questions?

Arching an eyebrow, I asked, "What do you mean?"

"You just look slightly amused, and slightly pissed," He added.

"Well, your daughter is a spitfire. The last thing I expected her to be doing was getting drunk and dancing out on the crowded dance floor." I expelled a deep breath.

He let out a deep almost contagious laugh—contagious had I had something to laugh about.

"Must've gotten that from her mother. She was definitely a get drunk and take off her clothes kind of gal, I remember the one time—"

"No. No. I don't want to hear about it…" I stopped him with my hands, really not wanting to hear about how Bree came about being made.

"Still, the woman was feisty as hell. She got that from her mother," he commented smiling at me as his eyes kind of glazed over. I knew that look—he was scouring his mind for the one memory he was most fond of. I did it, too. When I thought of my mother.

"I'm sure she did." I was never given the chance to meet her mother. Had I met her, would things have been different? I think so…

"You know, you and Bree aren't that far off from the same kind of people. She's lost just as much as you have. Maybe you guys could find the happiness missing in your lives through one another. I love her to death, but I don't think Jared and I loving her will be enough to hold her together…" James's talked as if he had experience with this whole ordeal. I wasn't sure I even wanted to ask.

"Well, if it's not you guys, it can't just be me," I

said without thinking. There was no way, after everything that had happened that I would be the person to hold her to the earth.

"Give yourself more credit, son. We all make mistakes and have a long past of shit always creeping up on us. You made choices and did things because you had to. Killing John wasn't easy on you, but losing your mother wasn't either. You have lost your whole family to death."

This man knew more about me than I was giving him credit for, and suddenly, I felt something I never had before—fear. Fear of the unexpected— of the future, and for Bree.

"You seem to know a lot about my family..." I blew out an uneasy breath.

Smiling, he said, "Yeah, I used to work for your father. Nothing serious. I never had to bury any bodies. He wasn't just my boss though; he was my friend, as well. If he were alive now, he would be very proud of you, Alzerro."

"Proud?" I stuttered over my words. That single word isn't something my father would've spoken. Even at the ripe age of five, I remember him being hard on me. Screaming and pushing me. A five-fucking-year-old kid… Like I knew better.

"Yes, proud, he would've loved the young man you hav—"

"That I've become? The person he wanted me to be?" I was angry, and as the air filtered into my lungs, I still felt as if I wasn't getting enough of it.

"Well, yes, in a way…" he added. All I could do was to stare at him, shaking my head. I was overwhelmed with the urgency to slaughter someone or something. Anger wasn't something I knew how to handle well. Lately, I was never in control, which made my life harder.

"This is the man my father would've wanted me to be, I'm sure…" I laughed, except it wasn't one full of laughter.

"All I meant is he would be proud…"

"Proud of what?" I bit out.

"You. The man you have become. I know your father wasn't a good man, but he loved your mom. Almost the same as you love Bree." Dazed and confused by his admission, I sat there shocked slightly… Was it obvious how much I felt for Bree?

"My father loved my mother, but not enough to end his behavior. In the end, he ended up dead."

"Listen to what you just said carefully…" he mumbled under his breath as he got up and slipped from the room. What was he trying to say?

Bree's words from the diner lingered in my mind. *"Everyone has a choice, Zerro. Everyone has a chance to change things for the better. Your past doesn't define you, and without a future path outlined, you're free to do whatever you want."*

It was as if James had known I needed someone to talk to… It was as if he knew my father's death could've been stopped had he made the right choice. Now it was my turn to make the right choice. Letting go of the Mafia was never a choice. They gave you options where I came from, but the more I thought about it, the more I knew I wouldn't have any other option but to choose…

I could continue down this path, or I could choose Bree. My heart knew what it wanted, but my mind told me something else. The day was coming…

My phone ringing in my pocket pulled me from my own thoughts, and as I stared down at the caller ID, my mind took a different turn.

"Devon," I growled. I was still pissed about what he and Bree had been doing. I knew he wouldn't hurt her, but the fact he had known where she was for hours before contacting me made me furious.

"Alzerro, you don't sound all that happy," Devon

mocked. I could tell he had a smile on his face. Asshole.

"What the fuck were you thinking? You should've called me right away," I all but yelled into the phone.

"Chill out. It's not like you came barreling down the street for her. She needed time to breathe. Even I could tell that," he replied in a manner making me uneasy. What had she told him?

"Fuck, I know. Why do you think I wasn't right behind her? That doesn't give you the right to just take her wherever. I was losing my shit, you're lucky you didn't find yourself on the receiving end of my blade. Until I got the text from you, I was contemplating murdering you." My hand was running through my hair so fast, I was sure I would be bald by the time this was all through.

"Tsk, tsk, Zerro. I call the shots. I'm the one helping you out. I had the right to do whatever I wanted. I didn't hurt her or tell her anything she didn't need to hear."

She didn't need to hear? What did he mean?

"What do you mean? I haven't lied to her about anything, asshole, and don't fucking talk to me like you own me. You don't. Have you forgotten I extended a leave to you so you could leave the Mafia? This is how you repay me?" I expressed my anger with every word. Who the fuck did he think he was?

"I'm grateful for all you have done, but you need to relax. I took her out, let her have some fun and that was it. She deserved it. After all, she's going to be put through the ringer next week."

"That doesn't fucking matter. Just know that she is mine. She belongs to me, and whatever the hell happened tonight will not happen again."

He laughed into the phone, and I was all but two seconds away from crushing my cell phone.

"From the way you fucked her against the hood of the car it didn't look as if you didn't want it to happen again. I gave her the freedom she needed at that moment and time, so put the caveman antics away, and pull your head out of your ass. If you want to take Mack down, you need to focus on him. If Bree loves you, she'll be here when the smoke clears."

What he said had slowly started to clear the fog from my mind, but it only helped a little bit. The jealousy I was feeling was hotter than the sun.

"Still, you need to leave her alone. As for her and I fucking, watch us one more time, and I'll gouge out both of your eyes with my hands." It wasn't a threat. It was a promise. Fuck with me and that was fine. Fuck with my Bree… and that was an automatic death.

"Whatever, Zerro. Here is the deal. I will come by and get Bree next week. Mack is on the lookout for you two. Hell, if he could get his hands on Jared or James, he would be splendid."

"Yeah, yeah… Get to the plan," I said impatiently.

"I'll come in the middle of the night, we'll scuffle, you'll cut me, punch me a couple times. Bree has to have some type of damage done to her… then I'll take her."

The idea of hurting Bree at all caused my stomach to flip. I never intended to hit her the first time I had. My mother had raised me better than that. Even if I was a stone cold killer, it was never my idea of fun to beat on women.

"Where are you taking her?" My voice came out gravelly. It was after one in the morning, and since James had slipped off the bed, it was just me.

"Don't act dumb. I'm taking her to Mack. I'll make sure he doesn't touch her or anything." Devon sounded convincing, but nothing was more important to me than her safety. In the end, if I didn't pick the right path, I knew I would have to let her go.

"I'm not acting dumb, I just wanted to fucking know where she was going." I wanted to snap his neck for talking down to me. He wasn't above me and we both knew it.

"You'll find out. Just make sure she's prepared. After talking to her tonight, she's not nearly as naïve as I thought she would be. Seems you have trained her far better than the other women you are known to be with." The way he compared her to other women I had slept with caused my chest to hurt. She was nothing like those women.

"You're right. She's nowhere as dumb as those other women were. She could stand on her own two fucking feet. Now, if you would like to keep that tongue of yours in your mouth, I'd shut it. As you know, I have a habit of cutting tongues out," I threatened before hanging up the phone. It hit the floor with a thud, and I had no intentions of picking it up. My mind was all over the place.

Clutching my head in my hands, I bent over... I was angry with myself for feeling as if I wasn't strong enough to do this. It was more than just a war with Mack or John. It was a war with myself. To be the man I needed to be or be the man she needed me to be. At the end of our story, I wasn't sure we would live happily ever after.

I involuntarily kicked the table with my leg, anger and frustrations boiling over. I couldn't do this. Never in a million years did I ever think I would be weak, that I, the King, would fall to his knees. When you live a life like mine, you know nothing but strength and power, and without either, I feel lesser than less.

With all my strength, I shoved from the sofa, my mind blazing with things I couldn't control. Was loving her really making me weak, or was it me bringing myself down?

"You're what you make of yourself, Alzerro..." My mother whispered in my ear as she ran her fingers through my hair.

I can't do this, Mom. I can't fucking do this... My chest was heaving, and as I whipped open the back door to run, I realized I had nowhere to go. I was that little boy again, trapped and afraid.

"*You're stronger than this, Figlio... You can do this. I believe in you.*" *Her voice was a mere whisper in my mind, rattling my heart so much so making me feel as if I would pass out at any point in time. Instead, I sunk to my knees in the back yard. The darkness encompassed me, and it was a welcoming feeling.*

"*Come on, Alzerro. We must be going now,*" *my mother yelled up the stairs. She was always telling me what to do. Sometimes I wore the wrong shoes or the tie I had on didn't look good. She wanted me to be perfect... but for what?*

"*Mom, I don't want to go,*" *I bellowed. Whining never did me any good anyway. Why I was trying it now, I didn't know.*

Looking me straight in the eyes, she smiled. It was breathtaking, beautiful in its own way.

"*We all do lots of things we don't want to, Alzerro. That's the lesson in life. Sometimes things are hard, and it's impossible to see the light at the end of the tunnel,*" *she said adjusting my tie like I knew she would.*

"*But, once you reach the end of the tunnel, you can look back and say 'that wasn't so hard, now was it?'*" *she added.*

I pondered what she said for a moment before asking my own questions... "*Have you ever had to do something like that?*"

Her head tipped to the side as she examined her work, and for a second, I thought she wouldn't answer me. Then she bent down to my eye level and stared at me for a moment.

"*We all have things we don't want to do. I have done my fair share of things I never wanted to do, as has many of the people around you. There will come a time in your own life when you have to make choices and do things you don't want to do. When the chance arises, grab it and hold on. You will come out a new person in the end."*

The memory spiraled out before I could finish my thought, and I came to my senses feeling the plush grass beneath my hands. Tears streaked down my face without will, and as I wiped them away, more appeared.

There was no other way around all of this. I knew in the end, the choice between Bree and I had already been made. The woman had my heart from the start, and I knew there was no going back. In the end, I would give up the Mafia for the woman I loved. Or die trying...

Inevitable

chapter sixteen

Mack

"Bree and I became well acquainted at the club before Alzerro had the chance to interrupt things," Devon expressed in a delighted manner. His eyes were shining so bright, I knew the idea of getting his hands bloody was all he was thinking about. Aside from that though, she wasn't with him, and that was a fucking problem.

"You had a chance to take her, and you didn't?" I shouted, pounding my fist on the table. The bitch was right within our grasps and yet he had allowed her to slip away. He better have a good fucking reason.

"I have a plan, Mack. Let me worry about working it all out, and you worry about how you're going to kill Alzerro." The way he talked to me had me wanting to put a bullet through his head. I had to stop the impulse to pick up my gun and pull the trigger. The satisfaction of making Alzerro bleed would be well worth it though.

"Never talk back to me again, do you understand? I'm your boss now," I growled, looking him straight in the eyes so he knew I was serious. I might need him breathing, but that didn't mean he couldn't be injured.

"Yes, we're clear," he said, smoothly taking the seat across from me. My mind drifted back to Alzerro, my hate for him stirring the fire in my chest. I hated him with a passion nothing could rival. He had everything I didn't; he took from me without a word, a simple thank you never passing his lips. Most would call it jealousy, but I was far from jealous. I didn't want just what he had, I wanted so much more. I wanted the empire, the money, the authority, and once he was dead, it would all be mine.

"Did you decide when you're bringing her?" I asked Devon again, wondering when he would tell me about this plan he was devising up.

He smiled smugly. "I had to do a little storytelling to Alzerro. He's a bit shaken up with everything taking place. He killed John, Bree's uncle…"

So, who cared? What was the point of being a ruthless killer if you had a heart? That alone is why I would make a better King to the empire than he.

"I see he's gone more than soft then. Bargaining for his life now, is he?" The thought alone had me wanting to scream to the heavens. The man expected us to praise him while he did things like this. No fucking way.

"Not so much bargaining for his but for his lover's life… I think he loves her more than he had let on. Taking her will close the deal indefinitely." Devon sounded full of himself, and I just hoped he was right.

"We can't just assume things, Devon. We have been sitting and waiting for a decision to be made. Your job was simple. Go in, make a deal, and bring her to me kicking and screaming… If you fail to follow through, I will kill you." My voice was cold, and I meant every single word I had said.

Again, he smiled, and all I wanted to do was to wipe the fucking floor with his face. Who did he think he was?

"Something funny, Devon? If I didn't need you, you would already be dead… Think about that for a second." I stared at him waiting for it to sink in, but as the smile stuck to his cheeks, my blood started to boil. This is how Alzerro had lost control. He wasn't stern enough. He wasn't hard enough.

Devon was stupid if he wasn't afraid.

"Boss, you must know something about me. I will take your orders well, but since this is my plan, I will run the show with it—"

Before he could speak another word, I cut in, "Devon, the last person who gave me an order was Alzerro, and you know where he is going. I had dealt with his ass for years, watching him take everything from me. He ripped my life apart and killed the one person I loved." I had spoken the words without even realizing it.

"What happened to her?" Devon asked, curiosity showing in his features.

My mind wandered back to a time when I was careless, loving, and even free.

"Mack. Mack." Delilah screeched my name as I pushed her on the swing. I had never loved someone as much as I loved her. She was only two years younger than I was. The Princess to another Mafia. I didn't care though… Our love had blinded me, and in the end, she had to pay the costs.

"Did he kill her?"

"He didn't… I did." Anger radiated in my words as I felt the urge to lash out.

"He made you do it, didn't he?" Devon asked, a little too eagerly, and that set me off. Right then I was a raging bull.

Narrowing my eyes, I gripped the table. Lashing out would mean I was letting him get to me and that what he had said bothered me.

"Enough about me. Let's get something straight. You will listen to me, Devon. In fact, fuck your plan. You have twenty-four hours to retrieve the girl, or you're dead. A bullet will be put in your head, and I will hunt and kill every single one of them."

A somber look crossed his face, and I knew I had him under my thumb. "Don't attempt to run either—I will know, and nothing thrills me more than the hunt for blood. Twenty-four hours. That's it." I stood from the table to get my phone. I had some calls to make. This little shack wouldn't do nearly as much justice for the carnage I was going to cause. No. I needed something out in the middle of nowhere with a drain in the floor.

Bree

My body ached in a delicious way as I rolled over in the bed. It was warm, which meant he had just gotten up. A smile pulled at my lips as I tiptoed to the bathroom. I could hear the water and see the steam filling the bathroom before I even entered it. My heart was beating out of my chest as I slipped through the door and closed it quietly behind me.

I was completely naked, and the thought of being with Zerro again so soon made my mouth water. The danger we were in only intensified my feelings for him. Every extra breath or day of life, I was given was meant to be with him.

I could see him through the glass of the shower. His head was downcast as the water sprayed onto the back of his neck and down his body. He looked utterly defeated, and for a slight second, I contemplated giving him the time it looked like he needed. In the end, my body won out because, in a moment's time, I crossed the bathroom planting my hand on the glass.

His eyes shot up, and even through the blurry

stained glass, I could see the darkness looming over him.

"What are you doing up?" he asked gruffly, opening the shower door slowly. His eyes ate up my body stopping on my chest before they landed on my eyes. His own were heavily hooded with desire, and I knew all it would take was one stroke of his cock to break whatever steely resolve he was under.

"I woke up and you were gone. I want you," I purred into his ear as I leaned into his body. He looked worn and tired, and I knew what we were going through had been getting to him. He was used to everything going as planned and protecting only himself. Our fight had been just that—a fight about Mafia being in his blood, and though I wanted things to be different, I knew they never would be. I would take him any way I could get him. Even if he was a ruthless killer.

He smirked at me, stepping back to allow me into the shower. Goose bumps spread across my skin as I came into contact with the hot water. I stared at him for a long moment before stepping up onto my tiptoes to land a kiss on his lips. His hands roamed over my body as if he were memorizing every inch of me.

"I love you…" he whispered… or at least, I thought he did. His words were so quiet a whisper wasn't even the word to describe it.

"I love you, too," I said back, pushing myself into him. His cock was at full attention, but from the molten look in his eyes, my guess was it was the last thing he was focusing on. Wrapping his arms around me, he sat me against the shower wall. Instead of holding me up, he separated my legs, setting each foot on the bathtub ledge. Then he bent down between my legs and buried his face in my pussy. There was no warning, and as his tongue, lips, and teeth assaulted me, I shuddered. My ass slid against the wall so much so I thought I would fall.

A shriek of terror was all Zerro needed to wrap my

legs around his shoulders, and eat away. Long gone was the fear of falling, and in its place, hunger so strong, it almost tore me in two.

"Yes… Yes…" I cried out, his tongue gliding through my folds. My hands found his hair and tugged hard as he nipped at my clit. The pleasure coursing through me was borderline painful, and as I came on his face, I felt as if he was trying to get as close as humanly possible to me.

"This sweet cunt wants my cock, doesn't it?" His voice sounded dirty and my nipples pebbled as small droplets slipped down over my shoulders and down my chest. Biting my lip, I nodded my head unable to udder a word.

"Words, Bree. Use them," he demanded.

"Yes, my pussy wants your cock," I exclaimed as two fingers entered me furiously. My body was just coming down from my first orgasm, and I was already in my second.

"More… More…" I cried out knowing nothing could do justice quite like his cock could. He owned me in more than one way.

"When I say so…" His voice held its own desire, and as I focused on him watching himself pump in and out of me, I became enthralled. Right then I came, my muscles clenched around his fingers tightly. Pulling from me gently, he brought his fingers to his lips and licked them clean. A thrill showed on his face, and then he stuck one in my mouth.

"Suck it," he ordered. I did as he said, sucking on my own juices. As strange as it seemed, it only turned me on more. He watched me through hooded eyes as I nipped at his finger gently, only to scrape my tongue over the bite.

"Turn around. I want to take you against the glass." He spun me around without another word pushing me against the cold glass. My nipples rubbed against the glass, and I cried out in pleasure.

His hands lingered along my hips as he settled in behind me. Anticipation ran rampant as I waited for him to enter me. Turns out, I didn't have to wait long because, with one fluid thrust, he was in me. My body shuddered, and I almost came from one single stroke.

His hand wove around me, cupping my tit as he rolled my nipple between his fingers. "You're exquisite, Bree. I don't deserve someone like you…"

He had no idea what he deserved. Pushing back against his thrusts, I moaned.

"No, it's I who don't deserve you." I barely got the sentence out as the air in my chest was heaved out as he pushed me hard against the glass. Every inch of my body was squished.

"No, love. I don't deserve you, but that doesn't mean I won't take you. You're mine." He grunted and nipped at my earlobe.

Without the chance to say anything else, he pushed into me painfully and pleasurably as if he were trying to rip me apart only to build me back up.

Tilting my head back, I pushed against him wanting everything he could give me. In seconds, I felt the distinct flutter in my belly. A zing ran through me leaving my senses fried. My breaths were pants, and as he slapped a hand against my ass, I continued to urge him on.

"Beautiful. Fucking. Beautiful." He somehow got out as he clamped onto my hips, bruising them.

Spurts of hot semen entered me, and as he pulled out, I felt as if I had lost a part of me. As if this was the last time I would see this man for who he was.

"Remember, no matter what, I love you, Bree. I always have, I always will. Okay?" His lips found my forehead, and for some odd reason, I said yes—not thinking this might be the last time I would see him alive.

As he dried off, I felt him pulling away from me. Why? I didn't know. The butterflies in my stomach just moments before were now replaced with worry and doubt.

"Are you okay?" I asked finally getting the courage to do so.

"Just fine," he said smirking. It wasn't a real one though; no, this was the mask of the man I had grown to know. I knew whatever was going on wasn't going to be good. In the throes of passion, nothing seemed wrong, but now thinking about it, it was. It was so different.

"Is something going on? You're acting strange... Did the plan change? Did I do something?" The horror of actually doing something wrong crept up on me like a disease.

"Just get ready for the day, Bree," he simply said, dismissing every single question I had thrown at him. Confusion wasn't even the word I would use to describe how he made me feel. Just moments ago, I had never felt so close to someone, and now—now, I felt as if we were oceans apart.

Slowly, I pulled myself together. I brushed my teeth. My hair. I was trying to mend my fragile heart so he couldn't see the hurt he was causing me. Whatever he was doing, it wasn't because he wanted to—or at least I would keep telling myself that until I knew the truth. A soft knock sounded against the bedroom door.

"Come in," I mumbled, picking up one my many books I had somehow managed to get here. It was strange how much pleasure reading could bring you. It could pull you from your current life and make all the pain go away.

I heard the creak of the door as my eyes lifted to meet James coming in the room. He looked wearily around the room as if I were going to lash out at him.

"Can I come in? I just want to talk to you for a second." He hesitated for a moment, which only made my curiosity grow. What did he want to talk about? I thought we already said everything we needed to say.

"Sure," I said smiling.

He crossed the threshold closing the door firmly behind him. It was then the walls felt as if they were closing in on me. John's death was still fresh in my mind and even if James was my father, it was hard for me to see things like that yet.

"I just wanted to see how you were handling everything? If you had any questions?" His eyes smiled. Literally smiled, as if he were happy for the first time in his life. I knew I meant something to him—that finding me, alive and well, was something he never expected.

"I'm handling it…" I mumbled over my words. How was I handling it?

"You know... you don't have to handle it alone. I am here for you. I want to be here for you, but you have to allow me to be."

I looked at him sideways for a moment as he stood in front of me. Was I really not allowing myself to let him in or to heal after all the damage had taken place?

"I know… I just… I don't know how to deal with all of this. It's like part of me thinks it's all a lie, maybe even a dream. Like somehow I'll wake up from it all and things will be different." I shrugged my shoulders.

He smiled softly. "I used to think the same thing when I found out your mother was dying. When I found out about you… My heart broke… To have something truthfully yours ripped from you." My eyes began to sting with unshed tears threatening to fall.

He knew heartache. His was different from my own, but he still knew it. It seemed as if we were two sides of the same coin. The same book just different stories.

"I'm sorry. I truly am. I never knew, and had I known, I would've said something. I would've done something. I loved John because he was all I had, but if I had known you were my father... if I knew your blood ran through my veins too, I would've made an effort to be part of your life." The words left not only my mouth, but also my heart as I spoke them to the father I never knew I had.

"I just…" He paused. "Now that I know about you, Bree, you can't expect me to not want… no, need to be a part of your life. So I want to try to be the father you need now. I know I can't go back in time, but if I could, I would." My feet closed the distance between us, and in a matter of seconds, I found myself in his arms.

I didn't really know this man, but it was evident he loved my mother. I could feel the love he had for me each time he looked at me when he thought I wasn't paying attention. I am the person they created together, out of love and for that reason alone, I know I have to try.

"I don't want you to not be in my life either."

"Then let's cover the distance, years, and months once separating us. Let's attempt this father and daughter relationship… I haven't always been the easiest to be around, I mean, just ask Jared." He sighed. "But I want this to work… Sam would have wanted that." The mention of my mother's name caused a shiver to run down my back. I knew in my heart, especially after reading the letter from her, she would have wanted it just like he said.

"So we try then." He gently pushed me back to look into my eyes. I think he needed to see I meant those four words. "You mean that?" he asked anxiously.

"Hey…" I could hear Jared's voice on the other side of the door as James wrapped his arms around me engulfing me in a tight hug. His hold was tight as if he was trying to embed an imprint of me into his skin—as if he might lose me again.

"Are you ready?" Jared asked peeking around the corner, hoping I wasn't naked I was sure.

I ignored him for a moment. "Yes, I'm sure—Dad." The words eased from deep within me, and I knew when I said dad now, I really meant it.

With one last tight squeeze, James released me with a smile on his face as he slipped out of the bedroom past

Jared.

"What was that about?" Jared questioned, his eyes narrowing in suspicion.

"That was none of your business, what do you want?" I changed the subject standing before him in a defensive stance. I still wasn't sure about Jared. Some days, we clicked and other days, we were like water and oil on two very different ends of the spectrum.

He watched me as I watched him, our eyes colliding.

"Right... Well, whatever it was, you're holding us up."

"From what?" I sputtered, clearly taken aback by his comment. What the hell was he talking about? I wasn't holding anyone up.

"From going to the grocery store." Jared sounded surprised, and I had no idea why. No one told me anything.

Huffing out a breath, I shook my head. "What are you talking about? I've never gone to the grocery store with you since we've been here. Why now all of the sudden?" It wasn't a strange question really with the way Zerro had been acting and now Jared raising my suspicions.

"Well, since Zerro decided he didn't want to do it, and Dad is busy, I figured you and I could go."

"You mean you saddled me up for the job so you don't have to go alone?" I asked raising an eyebrow.

"You know it. Now get your ass moving. Daylight is burning, and we have to be back before dark." Then, just like that, he slipped from the bedroom. I slipped from the bed. My boots were next to the bed. I had tucked the knife into my boot the night Zerro and I had sex on the hood of his car. I wasn't sure what he would think about Devon giving me a weapon, but I wasn't going to go into all of this without one.

Slipping them on, I walked from the bedroom ready to go. What I stumbled upon was an argument between

James and Zerro of epic proportions taking place in the living room.

"It's not your choice," Zerro growled bearing his teeth like a lion ready to roar.

"It's not yours either." James came back just as harsh, and for a second, I thought they were going to brawl right here on the living room floor.

"Just shut up, both of you. Don't kill each other while we're gone either," Jared said, heading over to me. It was then Zerro had taken notice of my presence. His eyes lingered on mine for a moment before going to the floor. What is his problem?

"Let's go." Jared more ordered than asked, and even though I didn't want to go, I knew I needed to get away, get out. Get some air. Clear my head and think about it all.

"You know you could ask me, and not so much order me. Just because you're my brother doesn't mean I have to listen to you," I enlightened him.

With a short laugh and shake of his head, he entered the SUV, leaving me to stand there and wonder what the hell was going on around me.

"Don't they have pads anywhere in this godforsaken store?" I mumbled to whoever was listening as I walked down the aisle marked toilet paper. Tampons were a bathroom product so what the hell was the deal?

As I searched the shelves, my eyes landed on a box of Kotex hidden behind a sign. Well, one box was better than none, I supposed.

Grabbing the box, I turned on my feet slowly, only to run into a firm chest.

"Oh, my gosh, I'm so sor—" My words cut off as my eyes ran up the body landing on two green orbs. Devon.

"Fancy seeing you here." His words were teasing,

but his eyes held danger as if at any second he would grow fangs and start yapping at my neck.

"Umm... yeah..." I stuttered over my own words, which obviously showed my nervousness. I had no reason to be scared of him before, but now. Now I was slightly frightened. It just showed how much a person could change in a days' time.

"We've run into some trouble, so I'm going to need you to leave the store quietly and come with me." He said it calmly, but his demeanor was off.

"What do you mean we've run into some trouble?" I wasn't stupid; the way he was acting made it seem like everything was off.

"I mean..." he said between clenched teeth gripping me by the arm firmly. "We need to leave *now*..."

Shrugging his hand off my arm, I shot daggers at him. "We don't need to go anywhere. When I hung out with you the other night, you were different. Now you're all uptight and pushy. What's your problem?" He was aggravating me.

"Bree..." He said my name as if he were pained by the mere verbal use of it. "We can do this one of two ways. One, you can come quietly. Two, I can take you against your will. The first way will result in little to no damage. The second, well... it might hurt a bit." I looked at his face to see if he was kidding, but he wasn't.

"This wasn't a part of the plan, Devon," I stated informing him how wrong he was. I was so caught up in trying to figure out everything as if it were a puzzle I didn't see Devon cover the distance separating us.

"Hard way or easy way." Those were the only words he said and my taking a step back must've been my way of answering, because not a second later did a white cloth appear from his pocket. In an instant, his hand was over my mouth and the white cloth cloaking my airways. My vision blurred as I felt a hand behind my head holding me up. Green eyes shone down on me and fear ripped through me. What was going on?

chapter eighteen

Bree

Light blinded my eyes, and as I tried to remember what had happened, my mind caught up with my surroundings. My eyes popped open revealing the fear I knew was on the other side of my closed eyelids.

A large overhead light was pointed down to me and I was chained to a pillar. What the fuck? The ground beneath me was cold concrete, wherever we were looked to be like an abandoned factory.

"Welcome back, Princess…" His voice spiked my fear. It was a different kind of fear compared to the kind you just thought about. No, this was a living, breathing nightmare.

"Leave me alone," I growled, feeling cornered. My insides spiraled out of control trying to figure out why Devon had gone against the plans. Why I was here early? And most importantly, did Zerro know.

"Leave you alone?" he said laughing loudly. His voice boomed through the factory echoing off the walls.

"Yeah, as in fuck off," I spat at him, trying my hardest to hide the fear from my body. At least my clothes were still on. He hadn't defiled me.

He stood a mere two feet away, and then, within a blink, he was on me. His hand wrapped tightly around my throat. I could feel the air leaving my body, and as I fought against him, I felt his breath against my lips—as he smelled me.

"You were always the best. The night I tried to fuck you and you wouldn't give it up to me... I bet you suck dick really well... I mean your mouth has to be good for something other than fucking spewing shit that'll get you killed." His hold released slightly, and I took the chance to take a deep breath, both my lungs and brain thanking me for it. I felt wetness against my skin and knew he was licking me. His tongue was scratchy and I knew the second I got the chance, I would cut it out.

"You behave, and you just might walk away from all of this alive." That was a lie. A big huge fucking lie.

"Don't lie to me. If I'm going to die, at least be man enough to tell me," I croaked out, even with his hand wrapped around my throat. I knew he wouldn't kill me. At least not yet. He needed me. He knew Zerro would never come if I were dead.

"You're right, who the fuck am I kidding. You're all going to die." He laughed heinously as he shoved me back. My body landed against the hard floor, and I stayed there for a moment trying to get my bearings and to bring oxygen back into my body.

"If I'm going to die, so are you..." I knew I shouldn't have said it, but I didn't care. The monster needed to know if I died, he did, too. I would make sure of it.

"No, sweetheart, you don't understand what loving that fucker has done to you. It's you who's going to die. I'm going to slit your throat right in front of him so he can watch the light leave your eyes. Then, when I think you have suffered enough, I'll put a bullet in your head and turn you into pig feed." His description had my stomach rolling around in knots on the verge of spewing all of its contents.

"Nice to know," was all I said. He must not have heard me because he walked away. My head lay on the cold concrete, and it made me feel better.

"You look like shit," Devon said, his voice causing me to squeak and sit up straight. I had thought I was finally alone.

"Now isn't the time for small talk. I can't even tell you how fucking angry I am with you. You betrayed us, asshole." I was seething. My rage was more than just angry. He had brought me here.

"Bree, just calm down. I didn't do anything wrong. I promised to protect you, and none of that has changed, all right?" He sounded convinced, but I wasn't. I knew better. Everything that had happened to me rubbed away the naïve girl I was before. I knew in the end death would be cast upon us all.

"This wasn't a part of the plan. Did you tell Zerro?" I asked, eager to know if he knew what was taking place.

"No. He will know soon though. I'm assuming my cell should be ringing shortly." Devon spoke nonchalantly as if I wasn't being held captive by a deranged Mafia lunatic.

"Perfect. Maybe you should've let him know about your changes before you just up and kidnapped me." I was exhausted. I wanted this all over, and even though I knew I had to be strong, I wanted to cave and to be weak.

"Shhh…" he said gripping my chin hard. Tears showed behind my eyes, but I refused to let them fall. Mack came into view, and Devon shot me a warning glare. A look that said you say a fucking word and it's your death.

"Was she smarting off to you, too?" Mack asked with a sick smile on his face. I wasn't sure I would make it through the next twenty-four hours without barfing numerous times. The man made me sick.

"Yes. She's defiant, isn't she?" Devon's voice turned cruel, and it was as if his own personal mask had slipped into place. Whose side was he on?

"Very much. Alzerro likes them sassy," Mack said, licking his lips as if he couldn't wait to take a bite out of me.

"I bet he does. He should realize she's missing here real soon. Prepare for him to come with guns a blazing." He laughed at his own joke, and Mack followed suit with happiness filling his facial features. What a sick bastard he was.

"It's just me and you. The other men will be sticking around the outside to protect the building. We'll know he's here before he even steps foot on the premise." Mack seemed awful full of himself. To me, it was too early to be boasting.

"A little full of yourself, aren't you," I growled. Devon's simple glare turned into a full on angry stare. I didn't care if it got me hurt. I wouldn't go down without a fight.

"Bragging isn't my specialty, Princess..." The words rolled off his tongue with ease. "You shall find out real soon when Alzerro the King is brought to his knees to watch you bleed out."

With anger in every word, I spat at him. "You're a fucking monster. A fucked up, psychotic asshole hell bent on getting revenge for what? Because you couldn't have me? Because you weren't born into the family? Tell me, Mack, what is it that pushes you over the edge? Did he fuck som—" My words were cut off as his hand came down across my cheek. A burning sensation radiated through my face and down my cheeks. I fell back on the concrete, my head hitting the floor like a bouncy ball. My mind reeled, as everything began to spin. I shouldn't have said those things. I should've kept my mouth shut because now all I would be facing was death—the dark, ripping your fucking heart out kind of death.

"Take her to the room. I don't care what the fuck you do with her. Rough her up, fuck her, hit her, do whatever you want with her." I could hear Mack's voice over the pounding in my ears, and as I stared off into the distance, I watched him walk away. His footsteps echoed in every part of my mind.

Then everything went black.

When I came to, I was on an old mattress in a room that smelled like dust and paper. A body lay next to mine, and as I rolled over slowly, I could feel my heart racing. Nothing had happened, at least not yet. My body felt okay, my cheek hurt like a bitch and my wrists ached, but aside from that, I was okay.

As I took in the body, I noticed it was Devon. His bright green eyes shone back at me. His face held no emotion, and I wondered if I was really even safe with him.

"I told you to keep your mouth shut. I told you to stay quiet, Bree. You didn't." He was frustrated with me, and I couldn't blame him. I was dumb to think this situation was similar to the one I had gone through with Zerro. My defiance would win me nothing.

"I'm sorry, I didn't mean—"

"Mean to what? Almost blow my cover? Are you crazy right now? I could've killed the bastard simply for hitting you. Instead, I had to stand there and do nothing," he said grinding his teeth with sheer force. He was pissed.

"I won't do it again," I said sounding completely defeated. What had happened to the strong woman I once was? Was I finally considering I might die? I wasn't weak, but merely staring down the barrel of a loaded gun. I didn't want to die.

"You're right, you won't. There won't be a second chance, Bree," Devon said blowing a breath. The room was cold, and a shudder ran through me as the air settled deep into my bones.

"What do we do next?" I was hesitant to ask if Zerro was going to come. I didn't know what the fuck was going on. I just knew he should've been here by now.

"Nothing. You sit here and pretend like I'm hurting you. It's expected of me. If he thinks I'm lying in the slightest, he'll kill both of us," Devon exclaimed examining me.

"How do we do that?" I wasn't going to let him actually touch me.

"Like this..." he simply said reaching over to tear the top of my shirt. Cold air hit my chest with only a piece of fabric draped over the right side of my boob. My shoulder and upper arm were completely exposed. Then he pulled out a knife, and I backed up, wondering what would come next. Instead of him turning the blade on me, he simply ran the blade against his own skin. Small, thin, pink scratches showed on his face and throat.

He looked as if I had actually attempted to attack him.

"Does it look believable?" he asked.

"Yes," I said, wanting to cover up. I felt too exposed. I was no longer safe here, and more than anything else, it terrified me.

"He'll come, Bree. He always does." The way he said it made me feel as if he knew Zerro more than I gave him credit for.

"How do you know? What's your past with him anyway? And whose side are you on?" I peppered him with questions, anything to get my mind off the present.

He stared at me blankly for a moment before smiling at me. He was so young, couldn't be much older than I was. How he had managed to get in the FBI, I didn't know. Nor did I have the intention of asking. He was a looker, and someday, he would make a woman proud.

"There is no side, sweetheart. Just the winning and losing. I go with whoever has the best fighting chance." As his words entered my mind, and I repeated them to myself, I understood what he was saying.

"You traitor. You fucking, lying traitor," I yelled, my voice full of fire and rage. He wasn't choosing a side he was playing both. The fucker was playing both teams until he knew who was going to win.

"Shhh…" he whisper-yelled, placing a hand over my mouth to shield any further yelling on my behalf. Instead of responding, I looked at him with the need to slice him open.

"I'm not a fucking traitor. I work for the good guys. If I didn't think I could protect you, I wouldn't have made the deal. Now shut your mouth before he comes in here," he said giving me a cold stare. Slowly, he removed his hand from my mouth, and the need to throw obscenities in his direction was large. Instead, I kept my mouth shut not wanting to cause further delays.

Minutes passed, maybe even hours, and slowly but surely, my eyelids grew heavier with every passing second. We didn't look at one another or even utter a word, and as I closed my eyes, and then opened them back up fighting sleep, I saw the genuine concern in his eyes. He wouldn't let anything happen to me. At least not yet.

"Go to sleep. If he comes in, I'll make up some lie," he mumbled, placing his head against the wall.

I nodded, leaning my head against the hard mattress. In a moment's time, my mind was headed to a place where death couldn't touch me.

Alzerro King's arms.

Inevitable

Zerro

"They have her, Zerro." Jared rushed into the house. His voice was full of panic, and as I stood there staring and doing nothing, I felt the guilt eating at me. I should've fucking told her. I should've warned her.

"I know," I simply murmured. I hated myself more than anything in this one moment. Jared and James's eyes both turned to me, fire deeply buried in both of them.

"What do you mean you know? You knew this whole fucking time and you never told one of us? You never thought it was a good idea she knew there was a change?" Jared was angry, and he had every right to be. I had put Bree in danger on purpose. And for what? The element of surprise.

"It needed to happen this way. If I had let you know, you would've acted strangely." There was nothing more or less I could say for them to understand. I had to do it this way, and it killed me. It would kill me even more to go in there and see all she had to endure because of me.

"Needed…? You're fucking crazy…" Jared aspirated loudly, his arms flying into the air. "I should've known. I should've known you never fucking loved her.

She was nothing but a pawn to you. Nothing but an inn—"
I couldn't listen to him saying things about me that were so
untrue. So I did something about it.

Picking him up by the front of his shirt, I shoved
him against the wall, getting right in his face. I didn't care
how we had been friends forever or that he was Bree's
brother.

"Never. I mean never accuse me of not caring about
her. Never accuse me of being anything less than being in
love with her. I would bleed for her, take a bullet for her,
and give my own fucking life just so she could take one last
breath if I had to. Never tell me I don't care."

I released him with a shove as I watched the anger
leave his face. Yeah, that's right, fucker, I love her. And I'll
do anything in my fucking power to keep her alive. Even if
it means I have to put her life in the hands of someone else.

"You—you should've told us, Alzerro," James
stuttered over his words. I was certain he was shocked as
shit. I didn't care if my feelings were known. I was an open
book from here on out. All that mattered was getting in
there to kill Mack, take Bree, and to run as far we could
get.

"Oh, really. Told you what? How I was feeding Bree
to the monster? Or if she died, it would be her blood on my
hands. Fuck no. I didn't need any more judgment for
having to do than I already have." I was fueling my own
rage as I spoke words I had kept hidden all day.

Bree knew something was wrong. She knew I
wasn't being me, and when I left the bathroom after
fucking her, I slipped into the old person I used to be.
Knowing I would have to do it again really soon made me
feel even worse.

"We're not judging you, Alzerro. Nothing of what
we have said is judgment." James was trying to cool me
down, but it wasn't working.

"It is. I allowed my mother to die, and I will not be

the reason Bree dies," I growled, my teeth clenching so hard I wondered when my jaw would snap.

"Bree is strong. She can handle this," Jared added, concern etched into his features. What the fuck did he care? The fact was she shouldn't have to be strong. She shouldn't have to go through all of this.

"She shouldn't have to, Jared. That's the fucking point. It's why when all this is over we're going to go away so she never has to face any of this again." The shock showed on his face and answered any and all questions I had.

"You're going to leave the Mafia behind?" Jared asked. The air was sucked out of the room as I continued to wrap my head around my choice. I didn't know how I would do it. After Mack was dead, it would be my job to rebuild the legacy, *or let it crumble...*

The FBI would be all over me, and I knew there was a small chance Bree and I wouldn't get a happily ever after, but I'll be damned if I didn't fight for it tooth and nail. She was mine. She was getting whatever she wanted.

"Yes. I'm leaving. I don't want in anymore." I threw the words out there as if I had a fucking choice in the matter. I knew I didn't, but I still wanted to address my choice.

"You know they won't let you go…" Jared commented with his stating the obvious banter. As if I didn't already fucking know it. But who were *they*?

"I'm Alzerro fucking King. I make my own choices. I don't need anyone telling me what I'm going to do. Stand in my way and you'll die." My voice was deadly as I slipped into the old person I was—part of me had never truthfully left.

"Where do we go from here?"

I turned looked to James. There was no way I was bringing him into all of this. Bree had already lost one father… She shouldn't lose her real one.

"You aren't going unless it's to drive the vehicle." My phone chimed in my pocket, and as I glanced up at the clock on the wall, I realized it was time to go. Six is the time we agreed.

Reaching into my pocket, I retrieved the phone. Sliding my fingers over the screen, I read the message.

Devon: She's asleep. Hysterical, of course. Mack's getting antsy.

That was all the message said. Not that I expected much more from him. I couldn't expect him to give me the whole fucking update in 160 characters. I wouldn't be okay until she was in my arms.

"We go now," I commanded. My gun was strapped to my side, and on my backside, knives were hidden where I could easily grab them. My black boots were in place. I was ready to take his heart and rip it the fuck out.

"Then let's go. I'm ready." I wanted to tell Jared he couldn't come, but I needed someone else. I needed someone to take her and get the fuck out of dodge if shit got bad. I knew it would—this was Mack, and he played nothing less than dirty.

I stood in silence as I watched Jared pull out his piece and place it at his back. He was trained well.

James slipped into his coat and out the door. For a second, I wanted to breathe in the air inside the house. Her scent surrounded me and invaded every part of my body. She wasn't just mine; she was a part of me. Her body lived through mine. I stopped outside the car looking at the house where, for just a small amount of time, I had a taste of normal life. I didn't know what would happen after all of this, but I knew if I had one wish, it would be to be able to come back here... When all this was over.

"Coming..." Jared questioned opening his door before hopping in the back seat. I nodded my head, jumping in the SUV as I told James the address to the place.

This all had to end with Bree alive. I owed her my life.

Pulling up to the abandoned factory, I sighed. There wasn't a car in sight. We were miles off a beaten path, and if someone called the police, I wasn't sure they would find us. Good, I thought to myself. So when Mack was screaming for me to stop breaking his bones over and over again, no one would hear him.

"Ready for this?" Jared asked as if he could simply talk me out of it. There was no way I was leaving her with that monster; after all, I had trained him to be that way.

Gripping my gun in my hand hard, I opened the car door and signaled for James to circle around as if he was turning around somewhere. Then I crept to the nearest door and busted into the place like I owned it. My heart was racing, and my palms were sweaty. I wasn't sure what I would discover—if he had downright killed Bree knowing I would come or not.

As I pushed through the door, my eyes took in all the metal beams surrounding us. Machinery was pushed out of the way and littered throughout the building. In the center of the room was a small body lying on the floor. Even from the distance, I could see it was Bree.

Her hair was matted, and though she wasn't bound or tied to anything, I knew there had to be a reason she was lying on the ground.

"Nice of you to join us." Mack's sickening voice sounded throughout the room as I watched him grip her by the back of the head. She cried out in pain as our eyes met across the room. Terror filled them and I almost slipped. I almost let the mask fall from my face, even just to give her a chance to see I was here.

Before I could even respond to him, I watched him

pull a gun out and point it at her head. She didn't move. Her eyes never left mine, and I could tell she thought this was the end.

chapter twenty

Bree

I heard the sound of a door being knocked down and then Mack was yanking me by my hair. My eyes focused on the figure standing across from me, and it took every bone in my body to not cry out in happiness as our eyes connected. His were void of all emotion. A cold, hard stare was all I saw, spiking my fear more as the hold Mack had on me grew tighter.

Zerro said nothing to Mack's welcoming, and as the gun came into view, I thought I saw a sliver of fear fill his eyes, but as fast as I saw it, it was gone.

"Come to collect your whore?" Mack's voice boomed in my ear as he cocked the gun against my head. I knew there was no way of getting out of it this time. This was far different from the time Zerro had held a gun to my head.

"My whore?" Zerro's face turned business-like as he raised an eyebrow up in questioning. My eyes lingered to Jared, who was standing behind and to the right of Zerro. Why would he bring him?

"Yes, this one right here, the one with a bullet cocked and loaded for her. She fucked Devon—you know that, right? You remember Devon, right?" The way he said it made it seem like he didn't know Devon was working with us... Or maybe he did. Time stood still as Zerro covered the distance between us. His eyes stayed on Mack—even though I wanted nothing more than for him to stare at me.

I didn't dare move. I knew Mack wasn't fucking around. He would shoot me at point blank range just to make a fucking point.

"Did he enjoy her tight pussy?" he asked smirking. My own heartbeat sped up as I realized what he had said. This had to be a joke. He had to be playing or something. There was no way he was actually getting 'buddy-buddy' with him.

"Well, not the reaction I was expecting, but why don't you ask him yourself," Mack said gesturing to Devon, who had just entered the scene coming through the bedroom door he had been keeping me in.

His pants were unbuckled, and he buckled them as if to emphasize he had in fact fucked me. I looked innately at Zerro waiting for something to show on his face. Something showing anger or rage. Something that said this was a trick.

"See..." Zerro paused looking down at me then to Mack. "She means nothing to me. Though her cunt is one of my favorites, she's not worth actually keeping around for a long time." What? What did he say? I was stunned...

My chest was shaking with every breath, and as I heard the words over and over again in my head, I felt the slap of them against my skin.

"She means nothing to you?" Mack asked as surprised as I was. This had to be a joke. My mind slipped back to the shower. The words he had said...

"Remember, no matter what, I love you, Bree. I

always have, I always will. Okay?"

That must be why he was doing this. He wanted me to make sure I knew, even though he was going to have to hurt me, he still loved me.

"Nope. Not a fucking thing. Now let's settle this like men." Zerro said as he dismissed me and the entire conversation.

"You're bluffing," Mack said. I could hear the smile in his voice as he pushed me forward and to the ground. My knees hit against the concrete so hard my teeth rattled. Tears sprang from my eyes falling slowly down my cheeks.

"Bluffing? I think you of all people would know if I were bluffing Mack." Zerro's voice was in full command mode. I prayed silently Mack hadn't called his bluff.

"That's just it. I know you. You're bluffing. I know it because I watched you. I knew the look you had in your eyes because it was one I had in mine not too long ago." Mack sounded like he was headed down memory lane, and I didn't want to hear about the carnage it took to make him so sick and twisted.

"Move on from it, Mack. I didn't know you were together. It didn't matter anyway. She had to die." She had to die? Who was she?

"You made me kill her, Alzerro. You made me kill the woman I loved. I pleaded with you to let her live, and you still made me pull the trigger." Mack was screaming, and I felt the gun at the back of my head again as he pushed it against my scalp hard. For a small moment, I allowed myself to feel sorry for him. A tiny shred of me understood his pain, but like I told Zerro, we all had a path to choose. He chose the wrong one.

"Love is weakness, Mack. You and I both know it," Zerro spat, his words flung hard at Mack. A loud laugh filled the room as Mack pushed me across the concrete until I was kneeling before Zerro.

"If that's true, then kill her. If she means nothing to

you, kill her. An eye for an eye as you always said." Mack quoted Zerro as if he had memorized the very saying. I looked up at the man before me, the dark shell of who he truly was on full display. I knew, if I didn't do something fast, all hell would break lose.

Dark whiskey colored eyes connected with my own as his gun came into view. He wasn't really going to kill me, was he? His eyes said he was sorry, but his body. His body said he wasn't. Killing me was a duty that needed to be done. It was then I made my final choice. I was stronger than I ever had been. With precise precision, I slid the blade of the knife I had hidden in my boot earlier down my sleeve into my hand.

"You know, even with her dead that doesn't change things Mack. You have to die as well. You betrayed me. You went behind my back and worked with John, who was my mother's killer. You told the FBI about us."

As I listened to what he was saying, I secured the blade in my hand. It was heavy, and if I landed it perfectly, it would kill him. One chance, that's all I had. Devon lied when he said I didn't have a second chance—he had given it to me. A small smile played across my lips as I waited for Mack to speak.

"You had everything I ever wanted, and you refused to pay respect to those who had helped you get where you were. I wanted my piece of the pie. I did what I could. Then this bitch got in the way and fucked everything up. You say love is weakness, but when I watched you look at her, I saw the same look I used to give Delilah in your eyes."

The words leaving his mouth were both vile and full of anger. I hated Mack just as much as Zerro did, but right now, listening to those words, I felt for him. I knew what had happened between him and Delilah was tragic. I knew it turned him into a monster the same way the death of Zerro's mother did for Zerro. The only difference was Zerro had me. I could save him, but there was no saving

Mack. He was broken beyond repair.

You can only be broken for so long before it gets to you—before the hate and guilt you carry around eats away at you. You could care less about being alone for the rest of your life because nothing matters to you. That's what happened to him, and I could feel it happening to me. Blood pumped through my veins rapidly, echoing in my ears. Everything around me became white noise. The only thing I could hear was my own shallow breathing. My hands felt like they were being weighed down by bricks as a thin layer of sweat formed on them.

This wasn't fear. No, it was preparation for war. For death. Long gone was the fear of my own death. Instead, a deep ball of anxiety formed in my chest. I was anxious, but I was also ready. Ready to deliver the monster known as Mack back to his home. To a place where maybe he could find his own peace.

My teeth were clenched together as I readied myself for the final blow. The savage desire to kill was pushing me to madness. The need for blood was overwhelming any further thought as I turned to face Mack. I knew there was a gun pointed at the back of my head, and there was a high chance I could die. It didn't matter though.

Everything happened in slow motion as I got my footing. I clenched my fist, my nails digging into the soft flesh as I formed a hard fist. With a precision I didn't even know I had, my fist landed hard on his balls. A rush of air left his chest as he bent over, the creases of his face filling with rage.

Without even thinking, I had plunged the knife upwards at the same time he had tumbled over in pain. The gun going off and his voice were the only sounds ringing out in the warehouse. My heart was racing as the bullet missed me by mere inches. I had no time for fear to sink in. I knew there was no going back now. I heard Zerro scream *NO*, as if to tell me not to do it, but I couldn't stop. I had lost my shit and nothing would tame the beast in me having finally been set free.

My muscles tensed as I applied pressure to the knife I had lodged in his left eye. His screams only became louder, full of pain and suffering. Blood squirted out, landing across my face as I yanked the knife out. I watched Mack fall to his knees, his hands covering his eye as if he were trying to stop the blood from pouring out in masses. When I looked at him, my mind went back to all the times he treated me as if I were nothing. I couldn't stop the urges flowing through me as I heard a little voice say 'make him pay.'

That's all I needed to hear. He needed to pay, and I was going to collect the payment today. I found myself walking behind him, my hand still securely wrapped around the blade. Coming to a halt directly behind him, my free hand snaked through his hair and jerked his head back. Whispering in his ear as I placed the blade at his throat, I asked him, "Do you remember all the times you threatened to slit my throat—after you fucked me, of course?"

My voice held so much pain I could barely recognize it as my own. A rumble sounded in his voice as I heard the mumbling of the word bitch, which only fueled the roaring fire inside of me. "Bitch? Hmm... I guess Zerro taught you something, after all, huh? Die with honor it is." Those were the last words I said to Mack as I roughly dragged the knife across his neck.

A gurgle sounded in his throat as I threw him forward with the little bit of strength I had left. Time stood still as I loomed over his body, blood covering his face and neck as it slowly dripped to the cement floor. I watched him fight to breathe, the rise and fall of his chest coming and going as fast as he could inhale and exhale.

A breath escaped me as I watched the light leave his undamaged eye. I had killed him. "Love always conquers, asshole," I whispered more to myself as I looked down at my hand covered in my enemy's blood. I think everyone in this room knew I needed to do this. I needed to be the one to take Mack out because no one tried to stop me. Not when I stabbed him in the eye and not when I sliced his throat.

I knew the moment his arms wrapped around mine as if he never thought he would see me again. His lips kissed at any skin he could get his mouth on, and I sighed against him. Relief flooded me and tears fell from my eyes. Happiness wasn't something I had felt for months, and with Mack dead, I knew there was a chance I could do this.

"Do we leave him?" Devon asked. This whole time I was convinced it was Devon who had been on the wrong side.

"Yes," Zerro said, pulling the blade from my blood stained hand. I shuddered to realize I had killed not one person, but two. This time though, I felt no remorse. Not even a morsel. Mack deserved death more than anyone.

"You gave her this?" Zerro asked eyeing the blade in his hand. There was a long far off look and a balancing of respect.

"Yes, I knew she would need it. I know you gave it to me for safe keeping, and I never was able to give it back to you. I wanted her to have it," Devon said smiling at me. I didn't see what the big deal was. We should be trying to get out of here.

"What's the big deal, let's go," I mumbled heading toward the door where Jared was standing. He then wrapped his arms around me.

"That's the blade his mother gave him when he was a child. It was his first throwing knife," Jared whispered in my ear. Realization hit me at that moment—the engraving on the blade said something I didn't understand. It was Italian. How did I not know that?

"What does it mean?" I asked without hesitation knowing Jared would know what it said.

"*Per il Mio Caro Figlo*," Jared said the words with elegance as if he had always spoken the language. "It means *for my dear son.*"

For my dear son. I looked back toward Zerro, who had tears in his eyes. I had killed the man who had been our nightmare with the blade his mother had given him. It was kind of like his mother had been here with us this whole time.

"We need to go." Jared interrupted the sweet moment his voice pounding in my head. I could see the flashing lights, which were basically right on top of us.

"I can't," Zerro said. There was nothing more in his words. Panic seized me. What did he mean he couldn't?

"What do you mean you can't?" Mack was dead. We could have our lives back.

"Someone has to pay for all the damage done, Bree. Someone has to turn themselves in." Zerro eyed me, his own face hidden of any emotions.

"You... You can't, you won't," I pleaded, fighting against Jared's hold.

"I can. I have to, Bree. I want you to live a happy and healthy life without a monster like me around. I have done some really fucked up things in my life, but loving you and taking you was never one of them."

I could feel the tears streaming down my face. "You can't fucking do this to me," I screamed, my fists beating against Jared.

"I have to. This is the only way you can walk out of here right now. So go. I love you. I love you so fucking much, but you had to know we wouldn't ever get this happiness, Bree." He was directly in front of me, and I wanted to reach out, even for a fraction of a second, to feel his skin against mine.

As if he could read my mind, he cupped the side of the cheek and kissed me with so much passion. Every word he had never said to me could be felt in that single moment.

"Take care of her, Jared," Zerro said pulling away, giving me one once over before he gave Jared the signal to take me away. I continued to thrash back and forth screaming. I didn't care if they found us if they took us in. I cared about Zerro.

My heart ached, and as I watched the last of his body move from my sight, it was then when I felt my heart breaking into a million pieces. He had done this to save me. To save us. Didn't he realize I didn't need saving—I didn't want saving.

"Jared, you can't let him do this," I pleaded... Mack being dead meant nothing to me. The fact the man I love was going to be taken by the FBI without a chance of ever coming out—that's what mattered.

"I have to, Bree. I promised him." That was all he said. And it was then I understood. He wanted me happy—I had found my home, my family.

"Please, Jared. Please."

"It's done," he said, his tone hard. He shoved me into the back seat of the SUV just as the first car came into sight. Holding me tightly against his chest so I couldn't move, I watched as the man I loved was left behind. I stared, watching until he was nothing but a speck in my eyes. Tears streamed down my cheeks like an endless river as I prayed they would drown me. Nothing would end the pain. My chest was sliced wide open and my heart barely beating. My chest constricted as I tried my hardest to take a breath, but nothing was coming. No air would enter my lungs and I felt it. Deep down inside of me, I had lost my very reason to breathe—my heart was breaking with every absent breath.

Inevitable

chapter twenty-one

Zerro

All I could see every time I closed my eyes was her beautiful face etched in madness. I knew her heart was breaking. What was worse—it was my fault.

"Mr. King." I was greeted by Zach the balding FBI agent, who had thrown me to the ground and put cuffs on me. Instead of returning the greeting, I simply stared at him in morbid stupidity. I wasn't stupid. Just because I gave myself up to these people didn't mean I was going to admit to any wrongdoing. *You did this for her…* I had to remind myself of that every hour of the day.

It had only been five days, but I was still struggling, wondering if I would ever get out of here and if I would somehow forget how her face looked.

"One way or another you're going to have to talk," he reminded me, yet again. This was the fifth day of interrogations, and let me tell you, they weren't above physical abuse—but neither was I.

"Talking would mean I had something to talk about…" I said my voice hushed before pausing so I could lean across the table. "And we both know I have nothing to talk about."

Instead of turning away as most grown men would, he just stared back at me, a glint of amusement in his eyes.

"You want out of here, and that's only possible by talking."

He was lying. They didn't want me to go. They pined to get to me for years. I had done some really bad shit before meeting Bree. I wanted to put it behind me, but not if it left me locked up in prison for life.

"I'm not a pig, and even if I were, I wouldn't have shit to say." I wasn't snide and I chose my words carefully. The problem was every minute I was gone was another stab to my beating heart.

"Mack…." Zach said… The name rolling off his tongue as if he has uttered the one single word more than once. Which I knew was true. They had him—or did before Bree plunged a knife into his chest.

"What about him?" I asked voiding my face of all emotion.

"Don't you find it slightly strange the man was found dead in your presence? You knew he was going to come to us and bring you in—but suddenly, he's dead?" Was he baiting me?

I wasn't sure how to answer the question. Devon had told me to lie, to plead the fifth, and no matter what, say nothing. He was taking the fault for Mack's death, but we all knew they would do whatever they could to pin it on me. Anything to keep me in this hell hole.

"I think Mack had death coming long before he started with me." Which was the truth. Mack was bad before he met up with me before I brought him to the group. The death of Delilah wasn't my fault. Her family borrowed money from mine. With no form of payment, their lives were taken.

Zach scratched at his chin as if he were thinking. His dark eyes hid whatever it was he was pondering.

"Let's cut to the chase really… See, you and I both know we have nothing on you. Though you were there with Mack when Devon killed him, we believe there may have been other motives. Mack came to us with the intentions of bringing you in, but after talking with Devon, it seems he might have rather have had you dead, instead."

"Well, if you have no proof, you should probably release me then," I countered, leaning back into the metal folding chair casually. There was some proof though, somewhere. I mean, after all, I had killed John. Devon took the fault for his death, as well, pulling the wool right over their eyes.

"Oh, you'll be leaving—just under different circumstances." The way he said it actually caused fear to bloom in my body. There would be conditions I was certain. Conditions rendering me from doing anything.

Before I had the chance to respond back, he walked to one of the doors and opened it. One the other side, I could see Devon's smug face. How had that man made it in the FBI for so long? Better yet, how did I handle hanging around him?

"Meet your new partner, Mr. King."

"My new partner?" What did he mean?

"Yup. You can leave this compound under the stipulations you join the gang related task force." I pondered what he said a moment. A task force? Gang related? Was I taking my own people down?

"What am I going to be doing?"

I watched as Zach turned to smile at Devon. He was lacking the amusement Zach had and that told me I wasn't going to enjoy this.

"We know you've done some really bad stuff. Even if we don't have the proof, we have the knowledge. Better yet, you have the knowledge…" He pointed at me. "With your information and knowledge of the Mafia, we can take down others who are headed down similar paths. Many do far worse than what you're known for doing."

I nodded, understanding what he was saying. I knew what they were talking about. Luccio's family, before I came into contact with them, ended up being in the business of human trafficking.

"Basically, I get to play good cop?"

"Yes, Devon here will train you on the job. You will report to me once a week. We will have a new job for you every week. Eventually, we'll get to the big stuff," Zach said, not sounding as happy as he was before. Maybe it was because I was smiling, and he didn't expect it—or he finally realized allowing a criminal into a branch of the FBI was insane.

See, those who know me, know my hate for the FBI is huge. However, those letting me go means something to me. I had already decided I was letting the Mafia go. Since my hands will no longer be tied to them, I can start over. I can do better. Be better. Even if it's just for Bree.

"Okay, I'm in." I had acted before the chance was taken away.

"Good." Glancing sideways at Devon for a moment, he walked out of the room leaving us alone.

"Never would I have seen the day Alzerro King joined the good side," Devon said. He sounded astounded, but somehow, I had expected this to be the plan all along. I owed Devon quite a bit. He had saved Bree's life, given her a slice of freedom, and by giving her my mother's knife, had given her the power to kill Mack.

Laughing gruffly, I said, "I owe you big time, man."

"Yeah, yeah, you do." Devon laughed back. For the first time in my entire life, I felt the sun shining against my skin.

"Thanks."

"Yeah, now let's get you cleaned up and do some training so we can get you sent back home next week."

chapter twenty-two

Bree

I was over caring. Over trying and taking care of myself. Losing him was all that consumed me. It was hard to think about anything else when the other piece of my beating heart was out there somewhere. Jared was trying, as was my father.

They didn't understand. They didn't feel the pain deep down to the epicenter. Our love was built on fire, passion, betrayal, and hate. We might not have been meant to be together, but falling in love with him was the most exhilarating thing I had ever done in my life.

The debt is never going to be settled, Piccolo." My body shuddered as the memory of that very conversation flooded into me.

"Why?" I cried out as he pulled me closer to his mouth. His hot breath was on my face, and he smelled like bourbon and man. Sweat still lined his brow, and blood seeped through the bandage on his shoulder.

"Because now it's I who is indebted to you…"

This was his repayment to me. His way of thanking

me, by making sure I was free of the pain. I would no longer have to deal with the Mafia lifestyle. I would no longer have to fear for my life. What he took with all of it was himself—he removed himself from all of it.

"Come on, Bree. You can't spend the rest of your life in this bedroom," Jared spoke from the doorjamb.

Burying myself deeper into the pillow, I screamed. I wanted to hurt someone. Something. Anything to help dull the pain slicing through my chest. People said time heals all wounds, but I think it's a lie. Wounds don't heal. We just learned to deal with the pain of losing them differently.

"Jared, I will pull a fucking knife on you if you come in here and tell me what to do again." I had no filter. I had no reason to care if I hurt others. I was out of control. Like a feral animal, I would attack anything or anyone who got too close.

"You don't scare me... I care about you, and even though I know he's gone, you have to carry—"

"Shut up," I growled not wanting to hear him. I didn't want the words to be said simply because it made the ache in my chest worse. Nothing made it more apparent than having the truth spoken, and I wasn't ready to face the truth.

"God, Bree. It's been two fucking weeks," Jared all but screamed, his temper rising with every word.

"Two weeks, Jared. Do you hear yourself? Two fucking weeks since I lost the person who made me breathe. The person who I lived for." I sat up in bed throwing the pillow at him. He caught it with one hand, throwing me a dirty look.

"Look, I know it hurts but—"

"What the hell do you know about love, Jared?" I butted in not allowing him to finish his sentence. All he did was stare back at me. We both knew he hadn't a fucking clue about love—what it entailed, how it made your heart race. How it made your palms sweat, your eyes dilate, how every hair on your body stood when he or she walked in the room.

"One more week, Bree. One more week is all you get before we leave here and you get your shit together."

"Fuck you," I spat at him hatefully. I was an adult. I could do whatever I wanted to do. In fact, I would now. As I rifled around the bedroom for clothes, I thought back to the moment we drove away. I should've been mad at him. I should've fought harder. I should've made him leave. Instead of being mad, I wasn't. I was hurt, but I knew why he did it. Didn't mean it was okay, though.

I could hear the doorbell ring off in the distance. It distracted me for a millisecond. It wasn't Zerro. He would never come bursting through the door ever again. Voices sounded in the living room. Pulling my sweatpants off, I pulled on a pair of jeans and pushed my feet into my boots.

The voices grew louder until I decided I needed to see what the fuck was going on. My hands gripped the blade in my hand—the one his mother had given him. It was the only thing I had left of him.

I opened my door, and the sound of a voice I knew very well met my ears. I could already picture his whiskey colored eyes peering into my own. His breathtaking smirk, the way his muscles moved with him in an elegant manner. I shot off like a rocket down the hall not even caring how insane I looked. I wouldn't stop at anything until I felt his hands against my own.

My eyes met his for a fraction of a second, and I had my arms wrapped around him. I panted against his chest, happy tears falling from my eyes.

"*Piccolo…*" he whispered into my hair while cupping the side of my cheek. I melted into his touch as I sighed in relief. I never thought I would hear him say that again. After ten minutes of standing in the same position, I released him.

"I'm so sorry I hurt you. I'm so fucking sorry." His

apology was sincere and as I stared into his eyes, I could see the pain we both shared.

"Where were you?" I questioned right away. If he wasn't here with me, then he had to be somewhere. There was no excuse.

"I was being held by the FBI." He shot someone a look, and as I turned to see the direction of said look, my eyes landed on Devon. When did he get here?

"You were with Devon?"

"Yes. Devon is FBI. He was planning to take down Mack. I was being held for a bunch of charges from the past. They had no proof, but they did end up striking a deal." His eyes twinkled as he smirked.

"What kind of deal?"

Reaching into his pocket, he pulled out a badge. "You're looking at FBI agent Alzerro King, baby."

My eyes grew wide as I took a step back. He was an FBI agent. Zerro the Mafia King was playing on the right side of the law.

With everything in me, I jumped on him kissing him with a fierceness I couldn't contain.

"I love you," I said softly.

"I love you, too, *Piccolo*…"

epilogue

One year later

Bree

"Alzerro King," I squealed as I crossed the threshold of the apartment. It was covered floor to ceiling with various colored balloons. It looked like a rainbow blew up in our house.

Silence followed suit as I pushed the mass of balloons out of the way so I could walk through. What the hell was going on?

"You had better have a god damn good reason for all this shit in here," I growled. My hands were full of books. I ended up being able to take night classes at one of the local campuses. Though I was way behind on my past degree, I was able to catch up pretty fast and transfer credits over. It had always been my dream to finish my degree in nursing. I wanted to be able to help those who were the most sick. Healing them reminded me of my mom.

As I found my way into the kitchen, I threw the books onto the island watching them scatter across the marble countertop. Where was that man? Butterflies fluttered within me. Are James and Jared here? I thought Zerro had said something about them coming over, but being so busy, I hadn't noticed. Though we were busy—Zerro with the task force and me with school, we were finding ways to grow with James and Jared. After all, they were the only family I had.

A throat clearing behind me made me turn around.

My stomach was in knots, and my heart was beating out of my chest as my eyes landed on the biggest bouquet of roses I had ever seen, and the man I love was holding them.

"What is this?" My eyes were already filling with tears and I wasn't sure what was going. Things had changed between us. In a way, we became even more in accord with one another.

"This…" He smirked gesturing to the balloons, roses, and me. "Is for you. Since the day my eyes landed on the photo of you at your mom's farmhouse, I knew I had to have you. Even if it were for one little taste, it would be worth it."

Taking a step forward, he placed the roses in my arms. "From that moment on, you ripped me apart— challenging my every move, meeting my every step. You loved me, even when I thought I was unlovable and when I thought there was no way we could survive this mess."

Tears were flooding my eyes, and the emotions swirled within me causing my body to quake with need. I needed him like I needed air.

His fingers cupped the side of my cheek gently, pushing away the tears.

"I knew I would want you to be my wife the moment you saved my life. It was my duty to care for you, to protect you."

Was he going to ask me to marry him? I couldn't breathe my chest was so full of love. Slowly he dropped to one knee, and I lost it.

"Will you, Bree Forbes, marry me?"

There was no hesitation in my words. "Yes." And then I kissed him like I hadn't seen him in days. Like that first day when I saw him after two weeks of thinking I had lost him. Our love story was tragic and in ways, even brutal. Some would call it fucked up, but I would call it *inevitable*. We, falling in love—it was meant to be.

The End

If you feel the need to stalk me you can find me on:
Twitter: https://twitter.com/AuthorJLBeck
Facebook: https://www.facebook.com/Jo.L.Beck?ref=hl

To keep up to date with all book related stuff, please
subscribe to my newsletter: http://eepurl.com/2aydr

Read on for an exclusive sneak peek at Devon's book:

Invincible (A Kingpin Love Affair Vol: 3)

Prologue

"Dev! Dev, where are you going? You can't do this to me! Please, come back to me. I can't do this without you! I can't be alone—" My chest cracked open and I watched him take a step away from me. His face was etched with deep sadness.

"I can't do this with you. I can't be what you want me to be. I can't force myself to make this work. It's over." The words ripped through me as my mind caught up with my body. Tears stained my cheeks, and my body shook uncontrollably… How could he? Was our love never enough?

I wake up with a gut wrenching scream ripping through my throat. The t-shirt I fell asleep in was stuck to me, my body covered in sweat as I forced myself to catch my breath. Breathe, Teg, just breathe. But for the life of me, I can't catch my breath and a part of me doesn't want to. A part of me wants to stop breathing because then maybe my heart won't hurt. It wouldn't be a battered, damaged, lifeless, blood pumping organ only existing in its own personal world full of mayhem.

When they tell you about love in books, they forget to tell you not every single love story has a fairy tale ending. Sometimes, you have to jump through hurdles and go through months, maybe even years of heartache before discovering what love really is. They don't tell you about the nightmares that will come. The ones where no matter how much you try to reach the person you once loved, they get further and further away from you. And no matter how much you yell, scream, and shout out their name, they can't hear you. They forget to tell you how you will find yourself crying more than you smile and never feeling anything except the coldness surrounding your heart.

They say distance makes the heart grow fonder, but I think it just makes you think. Think about what you had with that person, the love lost, and what you could've done differently to save it. When I look back on my love story with Devon Mitchell, I want to feel more than just what we were. I want to know deep down we had tried everything possible to be what we were. This is our love story...

Chapter One

The Past (2007)

I would like to say I saw the end of us coming. That I saw the heartache and change in him months before the actual incident, but I didn't. For whatever reason, I was blinded by his love, or maybe it was so much more than that. Let's take a trip down memory lane.

"Tegan, you better be ready to go in five seconds, or I'm leaving you here. It might be your graduation, but no one is going to wait for you." My mother was, well, a mom. She didn't sugarcoat shit, and she most definitely didn't tell me anything I wanted to hear. Ever.

"Coming," I yelled, adjusting my hair in the mirror. It was the end of May, and though it wasn't hot enough to turn the air conditioning on, it was still warm. My thick auburn curls stuck to the back of my neck, and as I pulled them away from my skin, I wiped the sweat away.

Great. I was a sweaty mess. Excitement bubbled just under the surface as I put my cap on and sprung from the bedroom. For one fleeting moment, I stopped in the middle of the hall allowing all the feelings to sink in. I was a high school graduate, I had a wonderful boyfriend, and a new life was just within my grasps. I could see the future in clear sight. My heart was beating out of my chest as I started walking down the hall toward the steps leading downstairs.

"Tegan, I will not—" My mother's words halted as I came into her line of vision. She took me in, her eyes running over my cap and gown.

"You look beautiful…" She said softly, her motherly tone disappearing. I could tell she was proud of me. Words weren't needed when her eyes filled with tears. It was her way of saying, Way to go, Teg. You have defied all the odds bestowed before you.

"Thank you, Mom." I thanked her, not wanting to ruin the moment by throwing in, the 'I got it from you' joke. My mother was a single parent and she had worked her ass off to get where she was. Nursing school wasn't a walk in the park with a one-year-old. However, she did it and managed to get me where I needed to be. If anything, it was I who should be proud of her.

"Ready to go?" She switched the subject and blinked away the tears. Just like that, her walls came back up, blocking her heart from the pain. She had always been that way. Forcing herself to be distant, even from her own daughter.

"Yup, let's go," I mumbled, gripping my wallet. Even with all the events that had played out before me, I was still excited about this evening. Headed out to the car, I got in and buckled up. As I waited for my mom, my thoughts turned to Devon. I was more excited to see him than to actually graduate.

"You have all your stuff for your classes in the fall ready?" Of course, the conversation would switch straight to more school. My mother didn't like my... what did she call it? 'Infatuation' with boys—one in particular. She thought Devon was the devil, a man who would lead me astray and away from the important things in life. She had no idea how wrong she was.

"Yes, classes are done. I'm registered, I have the

dorm map, and I have everything ready. You sound more nervous than I feel," I remarked, rolling my eyes as I stared out the window and into the open field. It was a good thing I wouldn't be too far from my hometown. I wasn't sure I could handle it.

"I am nervous for you, of course. I know how different college can be, how leaving home can change your life." I couldn't tell if she was referring to her own past or my future, but I didn't like where this conversation was headed.

"You need to calm down. The only thing I'm doing with my life is going to college and spending time with Devon. I haven't done anything wrong. Hell, I'm still a virgin, Mom. If I wanted to whore myself out, I would have already done it." Anger was laced with my words as I spat them at her. I didn't mean to hurt her by saying such harmful things, but I was tired of being compared.

Her hands gripped the steering wheel harder, as she pulled onto Highway 80 heading toward the high school. The rest of the trip followed me in silence as we both seethed in our own rages.

By the time we parked in the high school parking lot, I was about ready to scream. The tension in the car was similar to wearing a turtleneck in the middle of July. Unbearable, itchy, and sweaty. I wanted out.

I reached for the car door handle, not even caring about saying goodbye. It wasn't like me to walk away from something without resolving it, but I had no intention of getting into this conversation. I knew Devon, I knew what my future entailed, and I knew none of her fears would become my reality.

"I just want the best for you, Tegan. I don't want you to end up like me, throwing everything away for some boy who never really cared…" I could feel the hurt in her words and see the anguish in her eyes. She was scared and afraid because, when she looked at me, she saw herself.

"I'm smart, Mom. I got this." I patted her on the hand, giving her a reassuring smile before exiting the car. I didn't want to have to explain to her how much Devon meant to me. I didn't even want to tell him how much he meant to me.

"It's about damn time you made it here. For a second, I thought you might miss your own graduation," Caroline, my best friend said. Her blonde locks were blowing in the wind, and her green eyes were looking down at me. She was tall for a girl. At close to five foot nine, she ended up being taller than most of the guys she dated. Me? I was a messy five foot one. Fun Size, as Caroline liked to call me.

"As if I would miss one of the most memorable days of my life," I joked, scanning the crowd of classmates for him. We were all standing on the makeshift stage they had somehow assembled outside.

"I haven't seen him yet…" Caroline whispered in my ear knowing I was looking for him. She knew my feelings. She knew what Devon and I shared was bigger than some high school fling. It was dumb to think someone was your soul mate in high school, especially when everything was so full of change.

"Fudge sickle," I cursed under my breath as I turned around to find my seat. If I couldn't find him, I could at least look for something I would find.

"Hey, wait for me," Caroline yelled as I weaved through the masses. Many of the people before me wouldn't remember me. I was a wallflower. I cared more about school work and getting somewhere than partying or becoming popular. No one told you this, but after high school, your popularity would mean nothing because, wherever you started over, you would be back at the bottom.

"Welcome Class of 2007. Please take your seats," Mr. Erickson bellowed into the microphone. People started moving around, and as the crowds cleared, I spotted him. He was just stepping onto the football field. His hair was sandy blonde and reminded me of the beach. His eyes were pools of emerald green fields. His scent reminded me of home, and every time he was within the same vicinity of me, I felt him. My body, soul, and mind called to him.

As if I were calling to him with my mind, he looked up from his feet, our gazes clashing with one another's. He sought me out, a dazzling smile conveyed on his face. He wasn't a prince charming, but he was mine.

"He's here," Caroline whispered into my ear as she poked me in the back. My last name was before hers, but it just so happened she wasn't too far off from mine. She was able to sit behind me.

"I know," I said back unable to wipe the smile from my face. The fact I was graduating today meant almost nothing to me. If anything, it was my ticket to freedom. My ticket to a better life.

I watched him as the rebel he was made his way up the steps. Everyone else was already seated, and as he walked past the front row to his seat a couple rows behind me, I shuddered. Mr. Erickson made sure he gave him the death glare for being late, and then the procession started. People talked, memories were spoken, but through it all, my mind wondered. I couldn't focus.

When the time came to collect our diplomas, I walked across the stage, listening to the hoots and hollers. My family might've been small, but they were loud. Blush formed across my cheeks, as I took my seat.

A vibration could be felt against my thigh, and I knew it was my phone. Looking around to make sure I couldn't be seen, I slid my hand under my gown and into the pocket of my dress.

Devon: Meet me by the bleachers when we're done.

It was one simple text explaining nothing. I turned around to find him, but he was already gone. Was he not staying to receive his diploma? As they called Caroline's row, and then the next, the minutes ticked by, and eventually, I texted him back asking him where he was.

A minute later, I got a message back.

Devon: Busy.

My heart beat was skyrocketing as anxiety filled my belly. Devon had a less than stellar track record. He was what many would call the trouble maker. He had plans to make a better life for himself, but I wasn't sure where it would take him. He had family problems, and I was worried it would lead him down a dark road someday.

As the choir sang, and the announcement of whose graduation party was after, the anxiety ate at me.

"What's a matter with you?" Caroline asked concern etched on her face. She had worry wrinkles on her forehead and it made me smile.

"Oh, nothing, I just…." Could I tell her why the man I loved was missing his own graduation? He was dealing with family issues so he had to sacrifice his own happiness for everything.

"What?" she asked, confused by my mid-stopping sentence.

"I'm just excited," I half-lied. As I waited for the ceremony to finish, my mind tumbled around. We threw our hats and then it was official. I had graduated high school. Then I felt something deep within my chest. Dread.

"We did it. We fucking did it. We beat the odds," Caroline, squealed her arms wrapping tightly around me. I hugged her back, squeezing as hard as I could.

"We did," I said back, looking for him again.

"Where are you going?" Caroline asked, my body moving of its own accord.

"Devon," was all I said. I would text her and let her know I would be at the party later, but right now, I needed answers.

Parents, fellow students, and teachers moved to the

stage or the front of the school leaving the football field vacant. Off in the distance, I saw him. His slender body was casually leaning against one of the bleachers as he stood underneath it. His faded blue jeans were worn and rugged looking and his navy blue shirt defined every muscle in his chest. He wasn't overly large, but perfect. His cap and gown were in his hand, hanging off his shoulder casually.

"Tegan…" The way my name sounded coming from his mouth caused my knees to grow weak. I ran the rest of the distance between us. His arms welcomed me in a warm hug as my body settled into his chest. Home. That's what this was.

"You missed your own graduation," I stated the obvious, curiously hoping he gave me some type of answer. My tone was flirty, but as I looked up at him, I could tell he was angry. His jaw was clenched tight, and a crease formed on his forehead. Okay, he was more than angry—he was pissed.

"Yeah. Family obligations. I didn't even get to sit in my chair for all of five seconds before I had to sneak out the back."

"Hey, it's okay. There will be more graduations and accomplishments in your life." I was trying to sound upbeat when in reality I wanted to curse the hell out of his parents for being so selfish.

"Of course, there will be," he said tensely. His voice was void of all emotion, and as I pulled away, I felt a coldness descend over me. The look in his eyes told me he was sorry, but he hadn't done anything wrong.

"Is everything okay?" I couldn't hide the fearfulness in my voice, and though words hadn't even been said, I felt my heart breaking, every beat a constant ache.

"You know I love you, Tegan." He was questioning me? One of his hands reached out, pushing a lock of hair behind my ear. His eyes scanned my own face as I nodded

213

my head to answer his question.

"Then you know most good things in life come to an end…." To an end? What was he trying to say?

"Most good things don't come to an end…" I repeated the same words back to him confusion lacing my words. I was forcing myself to stay in place even though I wanted to run.

"I want this to work, Tegan. I want to be that man for you, but right now, it's just not in the cards. I can't be more than what I am right now."

My breaths stopped and my heart fluttered.

"Are you… are you breaking up with me?" It sounded so cliché—how my heart ached, and how his words even hurtful, soothed me.

His hands worked through his sandy colored hair, and his eyes turned dark. The soft light that always made him seem lively left him.

"I'm saying you deserve better. You need more than just me. If I have to push you away for you to realize it, then I will."

I wanted to laugh, but instead, I threw my hands up in the air, staring at the sky. Clouds were rolling in and were heavy with rain. For some reason, it resembled the way I was feeling right then.

"You don't get to make that choice for me, Devon. I get to make the choice—and I say I love you and I want to be with you." I was pleading, and the fact that I was, scared me to the core.

"Do you hear yourself…" He laughed, but it wasn't a humorous one.

"You're eighteen, Tegan. You don't know what love is, and some boy with more problems than he has things going for him isn't going to hold you back from all of this. I love you, but I'm not stupid. This is me letting you go. So fight it all you want, curse me, hate me, hit me even, but know my intentions for you are only ever good, and leaving you is the hardest thing I have ever had to do."

I took a step away from him, his words stinging my every pore. What had happened to the man I loved? What had happened to us and caused such chaos to ensue? I loved him and I knew it.

"You don't mean that…" I stuttered, praying he didn't understand what he had said. He had to know this wasn't going to happen. I wouldn't let it.

His eyes turned dark, and with a clenched jaw, he growled, "I do mean it. I already have someone else. Being with you was great, but let's face it… it wasn't ever going to work out."

His words kept hitting me, slashing at my heart until it bled. I fell to my knees before him, and as I looked up at him, I saw someone I had never seen before. Someone who I didn't love, someone who didn't love me either.

"We can…" I was grasping at straws as I felt the tears leak from my eyes and streak down my face.

"We can't. There is no me and you any longer, no us. So, just leave. Leave me, leave us. Get out of this run down town, and do something with your life that doesn't involve me...and, Teg? Don't come back. There isn't anything here for you anymore." His words were final, and as he stared at me for a moment longer, I felt myself slipping further. There were no words to describe the sadness seeping into me.

In a moment's time, my world had been flipped on its axis. Devon Mitchell has ripped my heart out and stomped on it. The only memory telling me that what we had was real would be in my mind.

Between tears, I watched him walked away. His steps were determined. Somewhere deep inside of me, I knew this wasn't what he wanted. Somewhere, I knew he was trying to be the better person, but really, I didn't want nor need him to be the better person. He doing this just proved what my mother had to say was true— all men would weasel their way in and then break you, leaving you with nothing but the absence of them and a broken heart.

Devon had done both. Except his leaving me left a gaping hole in my chest. Nothing could fill the wound of lost love.

Coming Spring 2015

Add it to your Goodreads list now!

https://www.goodreads.com/book/show/24255746-invincible

acknowledgements

This is always the hardest part of the book simply because everyone deserves a piece of the pie. When I used to think about writing for a living it never seemed like a realistic idea. It just seemed as if it was one of those dreams you would never be able to reach. Then it happened, I wrote a book, and then another, and another and now it's like an addiction. In the last seven months since I published my first book, Bittersweet Revenge, I have come across some great people and some not great people.

I have had to learn that friendships, relationships and lots of different things are simply expendable. People don't always care once you get somewhere, some are just using you, and others are just trying to say they knew you. I have had a very SMALL group of people that have stuck through thick and thin with me. That managed to hold on when the road got bumpy. Those people are my saviors. So while this dedication belongs mostly to you—my fans. It also belongs to others that without, their help, their caring nature, I wouldn't be here today and you wouldn't be reading this.

To Brie: My PA, my best friend, my cray cray critique partner. You lift me up in the most of complete and utter despair times. You teach me to let go of certain things simply because they're not worth holding onto, and you remind me that this is MY BOOK as you always say and I can write it however I want. I love you for that.

To Angela: My formatting extraordinaire. You had

me at "You really should change that scene…" You have by far been my hardest, and most important critic. You brought me out of the dark and made me grow a tough skin. You taught me the importance of accepting feedback and dealing with it. I can't thank you enough for that. I'm not sure I would've ever published if it weren't for you. Thank you for being here for me.

"Dream Team" you ladies know who you are. From our late night talks to our snickers about a certain male author, I adore you guys. You help promote me and whore yourselves out there more than anyone else I know. You believe in me, my books, and I couldn't ask for anything more than that. I love y'all.

To my street team: Bad Bitches is what you're and what you always have been. Just know that I am extremely grateful to have you all on my team. After all, I wouldn't be nearly as successful as I am if it weren't for you.

To my fan club: Though this group is new, it has become one of the highlights of being a part of my team. Enjoying my books is just one perk. Being a part of the fan club gives you a chance to get noticed. To be seen, and for me to show my gratitude to those that support me and my career. If that is something you are interested in joining, please send a request to: https://www.facebook.com/groups/423116867836218/

To the blogs. Thank you to all the blogs who supported this book. To "The Hype PR" for getting the blog tour together and contacting people. Thanks also to everyone who participated in it.

To Jennifer, Tasha, Wendy, Brie, Melissa, Tina, Angela, Che, and Amanda. Thank you for being the crazy beta readers that you are. Your comments and feedback make the book what it is.

To Jennifer, Brie, and Tasha. Thank you for proofing the shit out of this book.

To Rogena, my new editor. Thank you for taking me on such short notice. You're a doll.

Lastly, and most importantly: to my family. To my husband and daughter. Thank you for supporting this whacked out journey. It is never an easy feat to have to watch me spend my days and nights on the computer. <3

Inevitable

about the author

J.L. Beck is the Best Selling Author of Indebted (A Kingpin Love Affair Vol: 1), and The Bittersweet Series. She plays mother and wife by day, and writer extraordinaire by night. When she's not writing or doodling, you may find her watching The Vampire Diaries, or The 100. If you asked her if she would be an author six months ago, she would've laughed in your face. She currently resides in the tiny town of Elroy, in the state of Wisconsin. She lives with her husband of seven years, and three year old hellion.

Inevitable

Sneak Peek of The Dream and Aiden Story
(The Dream Series #1)
By Pamela Washington

Dream

What does a girl have to do to find true love? It shouldn't be that difficult, but it seems like it is. My ex-boyfriend proved to me that all men are nothing but dogs- horrible, mean, dirty, nasty dogs. I thought he and I were truly meant for each other, and nobody could ever tear us apart. Well, I thought wrong. I guess that's what happens when you fall in love with your college sweetheart and plan to spend the rest of your lives together. Luckily, that was four years ago. I am totally over him now and know I will never give a man my heart again. Never.

After finishing college, I moved away from the cold, lonely world of Chicago and headed back home to New York City, the Big Apple. Now it's time for me to buckle down and put my hard earned business degree to good use! I am currently just an over-worked accountant at Sac and Goldman, but I have higher aspirations for myself. One day, hopefully soon, I will become my own boss and live the fabulous life I have always striven toward.

I've known since I was a little girl that I wanted to be rich and powerful. My parents always told me I could do anything I wanted to do as long as I had a great education, stayed focused, and worked hard. Despite my name, I am not a free-spirited dreamer; rather, I am a doer who makes my own dreams become reality. Yes, oftentimes I feel like I'm a walking contradiction, but then I remind myself my mom named me Dream because she used to dream about me while she was pregnant and knew I was destined for greatness! So, I have lived my entire life with my head held high, confident that I will one day be featured on magazine covers, and certain that everyone will know and love the name Dream Evans.

    I've had several boyfriends, but they were just was that: boyfriends! There was no spark, no excitement, nothing to drive me crazy until I met him - Eric. We met at The University of Chicago Booth School of Business. I was just leaving class, talking with a few of my friends, when I saw him. In an instant, I tuned everyone out and just looked at him. You know when you have that feeling like the world just stops and it's only you and one other person who exist? Well, that's what it felt like! When he looked up and saw me staring, he simply walked past me and flashed me a big smile that I knew had broken plenty of hearts.

    "Hello! Dream, come back to the world of the living!" joked my best friend and roommate Megan.

    "Oh, I'm here," I responded absentmindedly, not really here. I wanted to know more about my handsome mystery man.

    "Are you coming to the party tonight? You know there will be some hot guys!" Megan was always trying to hook me up.

    "I guess I'll go, but I'm borrowing one of your dresses."

    In college, I didn't have too many dressy outfits. I usually wore nice fitted jeans and a top, but since it was my first time partying with Megan, I wanted to do the right thing by dressing up. Luckily for me, Megan was a size eighteen like myself, so I could help myself to her incredible wardrobe. The rest of my classes flew by that day because all I could think about was him. I rushed back to my dorm to quickly shower and shave before I made myself party-ready.

    "Here, I found something for you." Is she serious? My eyes practically bulged out of my head at the sight of the dress Megan had in her hand.

    "OMG! This looks like it's way too short! I'm not trying to look like a slut!"

"No, you're trying to look available! And hopefully you can find Mr. Right!"

"I guess I'll wear it, but only because you picked it out." I took the dress and squeezed into it before I curled my long black hair so that it was flowing in all the right places. I applied some light make up and some red lipstick to go with the red heels I had from my high school graduation. I gave myself one more look over and just couldn't believe I was really going to wear this out in public! You only live once, Dream! Have fun sometimes!

"Really, Dream, come on! These tequila shots are not going to drink themselves!" Megan had poured us some shots while I finished getting ready. It was too late to turn back now. Nope, it was time to party and put my smile on!

"Yes!!!! Dream, you must have plans to break some hearts tonight!" Megan was so loud that I realized she had started drinking before me. But tonight I hoped to see one specific person, so I took a few shots to gather some liquid courage. Megan knew I couldn't turn down tequila.

We caught a cab to the party. It was at a nice, breathtaking loft. As soon as I walked in, I noticed the hardwood floors, ceiling to floor windows, marble on the table, and incredible view. It was packed, and I didn't even notice when Megan excused herself to mingle with the other dancers. I wasn't the best dancer, so I just hung back and listened to the music. I walked over to the bar and settled for some wine. I knew tequila and wine didn't mix, but I could handle myself. I suddenly felt a tap on my shoulder. I turned around and was excited to see that bright, million dollar smile.

"Hey beautiful, why are you sitting over here and not dancing?" I closed my eyes and opened them again. Is he really talking to me? Did he just call me beautiful? Okay, Dream, get out of your head. Mystery man coughed.

"Oh, I don't dance. I just came here because my friend left me no other options."

"Well, we are both here for our friends, then. My name is Eric Pepper. This is my loft, but I'm just hosting this party for my friend since I'm not really much of a partier. What is your name?" He smiled that killer smile, and I felt myself growing warm. It was then that I remembered I had decided to wear a thong tonight; there wouldn't be much left of it if Eric's smile continued to drive me crazy!

"My name is Dream Evans, and it's a pleasure to meet you, Eric."

I held my hand out for a handshake, but he grabbed it and gave me a tight hug so he could whisper in my ear, "I saw you looking at me earlier today... I know you're going to be my girl." He pulled away and tugged at my ear. I hid a moan that almost escaped my mouth. I grabbed my wine and drank it all before requesting another glass. Eric sat down on a chair next to me, so I took a moment to check him out. He had thick, wavy, blonde hair that I wanted to run my hands through and warm, deep, soul-searching brown eyes. Man, I could just melt every time he looked at me! He was wearing a fitted black V-neck shirt with some blue jeans.

"So, you think you can put your mouth on my ear and whisper sweet words to me?"

"Yes. I think and I know I can do that because you love it. I bet you that you're wet for me right as we speak." He had so much confidence, and he was just sucking me in more and more.

This was the beginning of the end. The way he sucked me in was how he broke me down. After the party, we hooked up and were inseparable. He spoiled me, and I loved it; but I got too relaxed with him, and that's when things changed. As we neared graduation, I didn't notice when he began ignoring my text messages or made excuses for everything.

The night of graduation, Eric and I had plans to go

out with some friends. I hadn't heard from him and was starting to get a funny feeling, so I sent him a text: I will meet you at the loft tonight. I love you, and I can't wait to start our life.

We had plans to get married after we graduated. I was willing to put my life on hold to please him and settle down and start our family. Funny, it sounded like a great plan when I was in love! I hadn't seen Megan since we had received our degrees earlier in the day. I rushed to get dressed and put on a low-cut red dress that Eric had picked out and paired it with some black Louboutins that he had bought for me. I checked my phone to discover I had no text from him. I assumed he had probably started drinking already.

I caught a cab to his loft, and as I exited, I started having those strange feelings in the pit of stomach again. I rode the elevator up to his loft and was greeted by I Love the Way You Lie playing quite loudly. Is he really having a party when we are supposed to be going to the club? I used my key to get in and was surprised to not see anyone. I turned the iPod off right away and called his name. As I walked toward his room, I heard Eric moaning and a familiar female voice. I felt sick, I should've turned around and ignored it, but I had to know. I had to see with my own eyes; my ears could've been playing tricks on me. I turned the knob and slowly opened his bedroom door. There, with my own two eyes, I saw them, Megan was on top of Eric, riding his cock. No, scratch that, it was my cock - he was my boyfriend! He was kissing her and pulling her hair when our eyes locked. He didn't even stop when he knew I was watching him thrust his cock in and out of her harder and faster. I just stood there, rooted to my spot, watching them with tears filling up my eyes! Eric watched me with those same brown eyes that he used to lovingly and adoringly look at me with. Then, he did the unthinkable: while he was coming, he smiled that fucking million dollar smile at me!

I slammed the door so hard it echoed from the silence. I turned and saw the picture of me and him during our happy days. I picked it up and slammed it down on the floor, feeling like the shattering glass was indeed my soul. I was almost out the door when Eric and Megan came into the living room. The look on her face was a mixture of shock and terror while he had a smug, fucking grin on his face!

I hopped in the nearest cab and went straight to the airport with only the clothes on my back. I bought my ticket and put my head phones on as Empire State of Mind started playing. This was my new beginning, and I prayed that I would never see either one of them again. I let myself cry and wallow in self-pity until I heard the pilot say, "Welcome to New York City, folks!" From that point on, I had a steely resolve to never love again and to focus solely on me and my career. I would never again allow a man to deter me from my goals. I wiped away my tears and held my head up high. I was going back to my parents' house to start my life again.

Aiden

Just what I need to start my first day at work - a flat bike tire! Ugh!!! My bike is my preferred transportation method to get to work. I could catch the train, but I enjoy riding my bike through the streets of New York City. It gives me time to appreciate my amazing city and mentally prepare myself for a stressful day of work. I was so used to having a driver growing up that when I learned how to ride a bike at twenty-one years old, I discovered how much I preferred it over other means of transportation. It doesn't bother me when people give me confused, wondering looks when they notice I'm riding a bike while wearing an expensive business suit. I know they expect me to be driving a fancy car, but I do what I want to do, not what others expect of me.

My mother hates it with a passion that I choose to ride a bike. I can hear her now, "Aiden, why do you like riding that bike? A car can just hit you and kill you. Then you'll never get married, and I won't have grandkids!"

My mom always brings up marriage and grandkids, and I tell her the same thing every time, "When I find the right woman, trust me, you'll be happy! I'm not rushing anything."

That's how our conversations usually go. Ever since my father died while I was in Europe five years ago, she has been pressuring me even more to settle down.

Today is my first day as a senior vice president at Sacs and Goldman, a prestigious accounting firm in New York City. I am only twenty-eight years old, so it's a huge deal that I have such a powerful and important title. I inherited this title from a man whom I consider my second father. My job is my life, and I do whatever I have to do in order to be successful. Today that means I have to ride the subway to get to work on time.

Arriving at Sacs and Goldman with just minutes to spare, I decide to take a quick walk around. Before I can get very far, an incredibly gorgeous woman grabs my attention. I am speechless as I take in her short black hair, black pencil skirt, elegant white blouse, and "fuck me" heels. I wonder if she works here, but I don't have time to ask anyone. I appreciate her beautiful curves walking into the accounting office, and I make a note to stop by there during lunch to do some further investigating.

I make my way to my new office. Aiden Goldman is in big, bold letters on my door. I sigh to myself as I shake my head. I wanted to use my real last name of Grant, but my mother wouldn't have it. I choose my battles with her, and which last name I used seemed like a losing one. Mother always knows how to turn things around so they're better for her, and I just wanted to begin my new position on a positive note.

My mother is quite persistent and doesn't understand the meaning of no. She searched for me in Europe when I told her I needed a break. She didn't care that I needed some "me" time to sort through some major issues. When her investigators found me, I had already grown my hair out and sported a beard. My mom demanded I cut my hair because she didn't want her son to look like a hippie. That battle I won, and I proudly keep my hair tied back and beard trimmed. Appearances are everything, after all. Pissing off my mother is just an added bonus.

I walk around my office and take in the big leather chair, oversized desk, and the magnificent view. I can look out and see the Empire State Building from here. I untie my hair and rub my fingers through my hair, wondering briefly if I made the right decision in coming here. A knock on the door disturbs my thoughts.

"Yes? Come in."

"Hi, Mr. Goldman. I'm sorry to bother you, but they are ready for you in the conference room."

"Thank you."

My secretary lingers at my door like she has more to say, but closes it quickly. I guess she realizes I'm not the usual businessman. I work out every day; it's the best stress relief. I have shoulder length black hair and blue eyes. When I walk into a room, I command attention. I guess that's my mother's influence on me. I have two personalities: my mother/business attitude and my Aiden/does-what-he-pleases side. I tie my hair back up and go to my first conference meeting.

"Mr. Goldman, we are so happy to have you back in the states," Mr. Sacs greets me. He is sitting at the table with my second father, the original Mr. Goldman. I am surprised he doesn't offer me a greeting, but I try to be professional and pretend it doesn't bother me.

"Thank you, Mr. Sacs."

"The elder Mr. Goldman is ready to take his leave today, making you our new senior vice president. We know you have been doing great things at our sister company, so we are looking forward to see what you will do here as well."

"Yes, sir. I was giving them a hand with a few things."

Watching Mr. Goldman sitting there being quiet is unlike him, and I am really starting to worry.

"Thank you and I look forward to seeing you at the company barbeque I am hosting at my house."

"Yes, sir. Of course I wouldn't miss it."

Mr. Sacs gives me a pat on the back before he says, "Your dad would be proud." I tense whenever my father's name is mentioned. I keep my emotions off my face and focus on what I'm doing.

"Yes, sir. He would have been."

Mr. Goldman follows behind Mr. Sacs and pats my back also as he walks out of the room. I breathe a huge sigh of relief when I am finally alone. Whew.

This is why I left New York. My father was the mayor of New York City and was the most loved man around. At home, though, he usually seemed like he was unhappy. My mother was probably the cause of it. She had the money; she came from wealth. She loved my father, of course, but she was always determined to have things her way. When he had his fatal heart attack, I wasn't with him. I never got to say good-bye or get one last hug. When I returned home, everything changed, especially my mother. Her determination was mixed with vulnerability while her hardened, polished demeanor had cracks in it, but she never let anyone know this. She protected and sheltered me as much as she could. I always assumed it was because she was afraid to lose me – we were all each other had left.

I walk away from the window. I need to bury these emotions like I learned in therapy. Aiden Goldman, senior vice president, it is then. I take a deep breath and leave the conference room. It's time to find Ms. Curvy Beautiful and make my presence known.

Add The Dream and Aiden Story to your Goodreads list now:
https://www.goodreads.com/book/show/24677830-the-dream-and-aiden-story

Follow Pamela Washington on Facebook:

https://www.facebook.com/Pamelawashingtonauthor